"You are a pilot?" Rebecca asked.

"Yes."

Sadness settled over her. "I once knew a young Amish man who wanted to fly. Is it wonderful to soar above the earth like a bird?"

"It has its moments. What happened to him?"

She fought back tears. "The lure of the world pulled him away from our faith and he never came back."

After a long pause, he asked, "Were the two of you close?"

"*Ja*, very close." Why was she sharing this with a stranger? Perhaps, because in some odd way he reminded her of Gideon.

"Did you ever think about going with him?"

She smiled sadly. "I didn't believe he would leave. For a long time I thought it was my fault, but I know now that it was not."

Booker stepped closer. "How can you be so sure?"

"Because he vowed to live by the rules of our Amish faith. If he could turn his back on God, it was not because of me."

Books by Patricia Davids

Love Inspired

His Bundle of Love
Love Thine Enemy
Prodigal Daughter
The Color of Courage
Military Daddy
A Matter of the Heart
A Military Match
A Family for Thanksgiving
**Katie's Redemption*
**The Doctor's Blessing*
**An Amish Christmas*
**The Farmer Next Door*
**The Christmas Quilt*

*Brides of Amish Country

Love Inspired Suspense

A Cloud of Suspicion
Speed Trap

PATRICIA DAVIDS

After thirty-five years as a nurse, Pat has hung up her stethoscope to become a full-time writer. She enjoys spending her new free time visiting her grandchildren, doing some long-overdue yard work and traveling to research her story locations. She resides in Wichita, Kansas. Pat always enjoys hearing from her readers. You can visit her on the web at www.patriciadavids.com.

The Christmas Quilt

Patricia Davids

Love Inspired

Recycling programs for this product may not exist in your area.

ISBN-13: 978-0-373-81588-3

THE CHRISTMAS QUILT

This edition published by arrangement with Love Inspired Books.

www.LoveInspiredBooks.com

Printed in U.S.A.

For my thoughts are not your thoughts,
neither are your ways my ways, declares the Lord.
As the heavens are higher than the earth,
so are my ways higher than your ways
and my thoughts higher than your thoughts.
—*Isaiah* 55:8–9

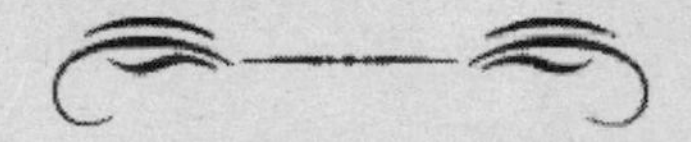

For my cousin Kay.
Eternal rest, grant unto her, O Lord,
and let perpetual light shine upon her.
May she rest in peace.
Amen.

Chapter One

"Booker, if you're gonna die, at least have the decency to go home and do it there."

Slumped over his desk, Gideon "Booker" Troyer kept his aching head pillowed on his forearms, but managed to cast a one-eyed glare at Craig Murphy, his friend and partner at Troyer Air Charter. "I'm fine."

"And pigs can fly." Craig advanced into Gideon's office.

"If they pay cash I'll fly them anywhere they want to go." Gideon sat up. His less-than-witty comeback was followed by a ragged, painful cough. A bone-deep shiver shook his body.

Craig took a step back. "You're spreading germs, man."

"So leave." Was a half hour of peace and quiet too much to ask? The drone of the television in the waiting area supplied just the right amount of white noise to let him drift off.

"You're the one leaving—for *home!*"

"I can't go anywhere until this next load of freight gets here. Then I'm taking it to Caribou." Gideon barely recognized his raspy voice. He sounded almost as bad as he felt. Almost.

"If I was sick as a dog, you wouldn't let me fly a kite, let alone your prize Cessna."

It wasn't like Gideon had a choice. Their business was finally showing a profit. A small one, but it was something to build on. He'd make today's flight. If his austere Amish upbringing had taught him anything, it was the value of hard work. "I've got a contract to fulfill."

Shaking his head, Craig said, "*We've* got a contract. I know you think you're indispensable, Booker, but you're not."

The two men had known each other for six years, since their flight school days. It had been Craig who'd given Gideon his nickname on the first day of class. Gideon—Bible—the Book. Hence, Booker. Gideon had returned the favor a few weeks later when their trainer plane experienced mechanical trouble the first two times Craig took the controls. Craig was saddled with "Law" as in Murphy's Law. If anything can go wrong, it will.

"Are you offering to take this run?" Gideon took a swig of lukewarm coffee from the black mug on the corner of his desk. It turned into razor blades sliding down his throat.

"Yes. Go home and get some rest."

Gideon looked at him in surprise. "You mean that? I thought you had plans with Melody?"

"We're sort of on the outs. Caribou in October will be warmer than the reception waiting for me the next time I see her."

A woman's voice from the other room said, "That's because you're a knucklehead."

Craig rolled his eyes and raised his voice. "Stop giving people a piece of your mind, Roseanne. It's almost gone."

Gideon rose to his feet. The room spun wildly for a second before settling back into his cluttered office.

Craig put out a hand to steady him. "You're grounded, buddy. Not another word."

Gideon hated to admit it, but he was in no shape to be in a cockpit. "Thanks, Law. I owe you one."

Craig leaned closer. "Roseanne is making me do it."

Gideon cracked a grin. Their secretary's powers of persuasion were legendary. She might look like someone's cookie-baking grandmother with her gray hair pulled back in a bun, but she didn't have a maternal bone in her body.

"I'll be back tomorrow," Gideon promised.

Roseanne came around Craig with Gideon's coat in her hands. "You will not come back for a week."

Gideon scowled at her. "Tell me again who's the boss here?"

Roseanne plopped her hands on her ample hips. "You two might own this business, but I run it. If I come down sick, we're really in trouble. Who can handle the computer, the phone, the fax machine, invoices, accounts payable and the coffeepot all without leaving her chair?"

"You," he and Craig said together.

Gideon smiled. "You're indispensable, Roseanne."

"And you're sick. Get out of here and take this with you." She held out a foam cup with a lid on it.

"What's this?"

"Your favorite brand of blackcurrant tea. I'd send some chicken soup home with you, but I don't have any here."

Blackcurrant tea had been his mother's surefire remedy for sore throats when he was growing up. He'd thought about sending her a box of this gourmet blend, but he knew she wouldn't accept it. Not from the black sheep of the family. Gideon was the only one of her five children who'd left the Amish faith.

As if his thoughts of home brought up a connection, he heard the words *Amish country* on the television. Glancing toward the small screen, he saw a female reporter, bundled against the brisk October chill, gesturing to a row of Amish buggies lined up behind her.

"Roseanne, turn that up, please." His voice was failing him. The words barely squeaked out.

She sighed, but picked up the remote and raised the sound level so he could hear the reporter.

"Preparations are under way in Hope Springs, Ohio, for this quiet Amish community's largest event of the year. The Quilts of Hope charity auction is being held here this weekend."

Craig moved to stand beside Gideon. "Is that where you're from?"

"Nearby." Hope Springs was forty miles from his father's farm, but Gideon had never been there. Until he left the Amish he hadn't traveled more than twenty miles from the farm where he was born. Now he lived in Rochester, New York, and he'd been to every state and all but one Canadian province.

The camera panned away from the buggies to a group of Amish men raising an enormous red-and-white-striped tent. After a second, the camera swung back to the reporter and followed her until she stopped in front of an intricately pieced quilt hanging on a display frame. "In the past, this event has raised thousands of dollars for the special needs of Amish families throughout Ohio. This year they are helping one of their own."

Roseanne said, "Now, that's pretty. I wouldn't mind owning a quilt like that."

The reporter ran her hand down the cloth and the camera zoomed in to capture the details. "Rebecca Beachy is the Amish woman who made this incredible quilt."

"It can't be." In an instant, Gideon was transported back to his youth when he had courted the prettiest girl in Berlin, Ohio. The girl who broke his heart and turned him down flat when he'd finally found the courage to propose.

"Someone you know?" Craig asked.

"No. There are a lot of Beachys in Ohio. The girl I knew would be married to some Amish farmer or carpenter." It was the life Rebecca wanted—as long as he wasn't the farmer or the carpenter. Chances were slim that it was the same woman, but his gaze stayed glued to the screen.

The camera switched to a group of Amish women who were talking. The women didn't realize they were being filmed. They were dressed alike in dark coats and bonnets. One held a baby on her hip, but it was the woman in the center that he strained to see.

The reporter's voice cut into Gideon's thoughts. "The money from this year's auction is going to help pay for some very specialized surgery for Miss Beachy."

The camera zoomed in on the group of women and Rebecca's face filled the television screen. The sight knocked the breath from his body. After almost ten years, his heart still ached at the sight of her. She was more beautiful than ever. Her heart-shaped face with those stunning high cheekbones had matured from the soft roundness of youth into a quiet elegance.

"Why do they wear those odd white hats?" Rose-anne asked.

"It's called a prayer *kapp.* Amish women believe the Bible commands them to cover their hair when they pray."

"But they don't just wear them in church?" Rose-anne turned to stare at him, waiting for an explanation.

He wanted to hear what the reporter was saying. "A woman might want to pray anytime, so she keeps her head covered all day. They never cut their hair, either."

Rebecca's blond hair must be past her hips by now. He'd seen it down only once. It was the night he talked Rebecca into going to a hoedown with him and his rowdy friends.

Hoedown was a benign name for a weekend-long party with loud music, alcohol and drugs attended by some of the wilder Amish youth during their rumspringa, or running-around time. He had made the most of his rumspringa and partied hard. For Rebecca, that one party had been her only venture on the wild side.

Gideon took the remote from his secretary and

turned up the volume. The TV reporter droned on. "Miss Beachy stitched this beautiful quilt entirely by hand. What's even more amazing is that she is totally blind."

"How on earth can a blind woman make a quilt?" Roseanne's skeptical comment barely registered in Gideon's brain.

Rebecca was blind?

Suddenly, he was gasping for air and coughing so hard his head pounded. It took a minute to catch his breath. Roseanne pulled the lid off the tea and offered him some. He took a grateful sip.

Concern filled her eyes. "Do you know her?"

"I once asked her to marry me. I think if she had said yes, I would be a bearded Amish farmer now." With a blind wife.

Rebecca was blind. He couldn't wrap his brain around the fact. Why? When had it happened? The thought of the vibrant woman he'd known living her life in darkness left an ache in his chest that had nothing to do with the flu. Before he could gather more details, the news program moved on to the weather forecast and warnings about an artic front plowing southward delivering early ice and snow in its wake.

Craig said, "I read the Amish don't believe in health insurance. Is that true?"

"Most don't. The community would rally round a

family that had big medical expenses, but they could only do so much."

Gideon had to help. He pulled his phone from his pocket and prayed the news station could give him more information. It wasn't until he tried to speak that he realized his voice was gone. He handed the phone to Roseanne and wrote a quick note on a piece of paper from her desk.

Get me all the information you can about the auction.

After a brief conversation, Roseanne hung up and handed the notepad to him. "It's at noon the day after tomorrow."

That gave him one day to rest up. If he headed out early the following morning he could make the six-hour trip there and back. It would be a long day, but doable.

Craig said, "Tell me you're not going to drive to Ohio."

Roseanne studied Gideon's face. "Yes, he is."

"I know we're going to have a wonderful time today."

Rebecca Beachy didn't share her aunt Vera's optimism. She folded her white cane and tucked it under her arm. Grasping her aunt's elbow, she let Vera lead her toward the tent where the quilt auction was about to get under way. Besides Rebecca's quilt, there were thirty others being auctioned off.

Rebecca kept a smile on her face as she followed her aunt even though she was anything but comfortable.

Disoriented by the noise and smells of the fair-like atmosphere, she wished she were back in her aunt's small home where everything was in its rightful place and nothing was ready to trip her up.

The thought had barely crossed her mind before something hit her legs and made her stumble.

"Sorry," a pair of childish voices called out. She heard their footsteps as the children ran away.

"Hooligans," Vera muttered.

"Excited *Kinder* at play." Rebecca listened to the sound of the children's voices as they shouted to each other. A pang of longing escaped from the place in her heart where she kept her fading dreams.

Dreams she once had of being a wife and a mother, of holding a child of her own. She'd had the chance to make those dreams come true years before, but she had been too afraid to take the risk. Had she made the right choice? Only God knew.

"*Englisch* children without manners," Vera grumbled. "Come, we're almost there."

Rebecca drew a deep breath. Her life was what it was. This was God's plan for her. Impossible dreams had no place in her dark world.

But if the darkness could be lifted?

She didn't dare hope for such a miracle. This benefit auction was her aunt's doing. Rebecca had tried to convince her the surgery was too expensive. They would need more money than would be raised here today. Even if they did manage to cover the cost, there was no guarantee her sight would be restored.

She had argued long and hard to no avail. The auction was under way. It was all in God's hands, but Rebecca didn't believe He would produce a miracle for her. She was not worthy. She knew exactly why her sight had been taken from her.

She pulled the collar of her coat closed against a cold gust of wind and ugly memories. An early storm was on its way, but God had seen fit to hold it off until the auction was over. For that she was thankful. At least she and her aunt didn't need to worry about traveling home in foul weather. They had already made plans to stay in town for several days.

Suddenly, the wind was blocked, and Rebecca knew they were inside the tent. It was warmer than she expected. The smells of hot dogs, popcorn, hot chocolate and coffee told her they were near the concession stand. The sound of hundreds of voices raised to be heard over the general din assaulted her ears. When they finally reached their seats, Rebecca unbuttoned her coat and removed her heavy bonnet. Many of the people around her greeted her in her native Pennsylvania Dutch. Leaning closer to her aunt, she asked, "Is my *kapp* on straight? Do I look okay?"

"And why wouldn't you look okay?" Vera asked.

"Because I may have egg yolk from breakfast on my dress, or my backside may be covered with dust from the buggy seat. I don't know. Just tell me I look presentable." She knew everyone would be staring at her when her quilt was brought up for auction. She didn't like being the center of attention.

"You look lovely." The harsh whisper startled her.

She turned her face toward the sound coming from behind her and caught the scent of a man's spicy aftershave. The voice must belong to an *Englisch* fellow. *"Danki."*

"You're most welcome." He coughed and she realized he was sick.

"You sound as if you should be abed with that cold."

"So I've been told," he admitted.

"It is a foolish fellow who doesn't follow *goot* advice."

"Some people definitely consider me foolish." His raspy voice held a hint of amusement.

He was poking fun at himself. She liked that. There was something familiar about him but she couldn't put her finger on what it was. "Have we met?"

"I'm not from here," he said quickly.

Vera said, "I see the bishop's wife. I want to ask her how her brother is doing after his heart attack." She rose and moved away, leaving Rebecca to her own devices.

The *Englisch* fellow said, "You've been deserted."

She heard the folding chair beside her creak and his voice moved closer as if he were leaning over the seat. Although she knew it was unwise to encourage interaction with an outsider, she wanted to figure out why he seemed familiar. She wasn't sure, but she thought she heard traces of a Pennsylvania Dutch accent in his raspy speech.

She said, "I don't mind. I'm Rebecca Beachy."

There was a long hesitation, then he said, "My friends call me Booker. The quilts on display are beautiful."

"Are you a collector, Mr. Booker, or did your wife make you come today? That's often the case with the men in the audience, Amish and English alike."

"I'm not married. What about you?"

"*Nee,* I am an *alt maedel.*"

"Hardly an *old* maid. There must be something very wrong with the men in this community."

Flustered, she quickly changed the subject, but he had confirmed one suspicion. He understood at least a little of her native tongue. "Have you been to one of our auctions before?"

"No, but I know what goes into making a quilt like the ones up on stage. My mother quilts."

"They do take a lot of effort. I'm glad people such as yourself appreciate our Amish workmanship. How did you hear about our auction?"

"I caught the story on WHAM."

Puzzled, she asked, "What is WHAM?"

"A television station where I live."

"There was a story about our little auction on television?"

"Yes, and about you."

She frowned. "Me? Why would they talk about me?"

"According to the story, this auction is helping raise money for your eye surgery." His voice was barely a whisper and fading.

Embarrassment overtook her. The heat of a blush rose up her neck and flared across her cheeks. "Perhaps Dr. White or his nurse, Amber Bradley, told them about me. I wish they had not."

"I thought it odd for an Amish person to seek publicity. The Amish normally shy away from the spotlight, don't they?"

"We do not seek to draw attention to ourselves. We seek only to live plain, humble lives. But you know that already, don't you? How is it that you are familiar with our language?"

"A long time ago I lived in a community that had Amish families." His voice cracked on the last word.

Sympathy for him overrode her curiosity about his past. "You should rest your voice."

"How long have you been blind?"

She was shocked by his abrupt personal question. Her reaction must have shown on her face because he immediately said, "I'm sorry. That was rude. It's none of my business."

She rarely spoke about the time before she'd lost her sight. It was as if that life, filled with happiness, colors and the faces of the people she loved, belonged to another woman. Remembering the way she lost her sight always left her feeling depressed. It went bit by bit over the course of three years, first details and then colors, beloved faces and finally even the light. God had given her this burden. She must bear it well.

Booker interrupted her moment of pity when he said, "I didn't mean to pry. Please forgive me."

He meant no harm. It was her pride and her inability to fully accept God's will that made remembering painful. "You are forgiven. I learned I was going blind when I was twenty. My sight left me completely seven years ago."

There was a long period of silence. What was he thinking? Did he feel sorry for her? Did he think she was helpless and useless? She rushed to dissuade him of such thoughts and repeated the words her bishop told her the day the last of her sight failed. "Do not think to pity me. My blindness has been a gift from God."

A gift meant to show her the error of her ways and lead her to repent.

"How can you call it a gift?" His scratchy voice broke. Because of his illness, or for some other reason?

She smiled sadly. "It is a struggle sometimes, but I know all that God gives us, whether hardship or happiness, is in some way a gift. We learn more about ourselves, and about how much we need God, during times of sorrow than we do in times of joy. I accept my life for what it is." At least, she tried.

"But this surgery, it can restore your sight?"

"If God wills it."

"Don't you mean if the surgeon is skilled enough?"

"God's miracles come in many forms. If my sight is restored by the skill of an *Englisch* doctor or by a flash of lightning it is all the work of God."

"Then I pray He will be merciful. I wish you the very best, Rebecca Beachy."

She heard his chair scoot back, then the sound of his footsteps until they blended into the hum of activity and voices inside the tent. A sharp sense of loss filled her but she didn't understand why.

A few moments later, her aunt returned and sat down. Rebecca's hand found Vera's sleeve. "*Aenti,* do you know the man that was just sitting here?"

"What man?"

"He was sitting in the row behind us. He's *Englisch.*"

"There are many *Englisch* here. I didn't pay attention."

"I thought perhaps he was someone I should know, but I didn't recognize his name. He called himself Booker."

"I don't know anyone by that name. The bidding

is getting ready to start. I pray your quilt does well. It's lovely."

"You picked the material. I merely stitched it together."

Her aunt's hands were twisted and gnarled with arthritis, making sewing and many daily tasks impossible for her. It was one reason why Rebecca chose to live with her aunt when her vision began to fade. She knew she could always be useful in her aunt's household.

Vera said, "I do wish you had put your Christmas Star quilt in the auction today. I'm sure it would fetch a fine price and we could use the money."

"I don't wish to sell that one, *Aenti.* It will be a gift when it is done."

There was something special about the quilt she had been working on for the past several weeks. Something in the feel of the fabrics, the way the seams lay straight and true with so little effort. Her Christmas quilt would not be for sale. It would be a gift for a wedding or for someone's birthday. She didn't know who would receive it. God would show her in His own time.

Vera patted Rebecca's hand. "Anyone that receives such a gift will be blessed. I pray it is God's will to heal you, child. I pray that one day you may see with your own eyes the beauty you have crafted."

Chapter Two

Rebecca was still the loveliest woman Gideon had ever laid eyes on, and she had lied to him.

Seeing her in person, it was as if a single day had passed—not ten years. Feelings he thought long dead and buried rushed to life, leaving him shaken. Coming here had been a bad idea.

He stood near the back of the tent where he could keep an eye on Rebecca and the auction proceedings as he pondered the stunning information she'd revealed. The noise of the crowd, the chanting voice of the auctioneer, the shouts of his helpers as they spotted raised hands in the audience, all faded into a rumbling background for Gideon's whirling mind.

She obviously had no idea who he was, and he needed to keep it that way. His missing voice was a blessing in disguise. If she knew who he was, she wouldn't have spoken to him at all.

Because he had been baptized prior to leaving

the faith he had been placed under the *Meidung,* the ban, making contact with his Amish family and friends impossible unless he publicly repented and asked for the church's forgiveness. Bidding for Rebecca's quilt at this auction would be his roundabout way of giving aid she could accept.

By leaving the faith after making his vows he had cut himself off completely from everything he'd known. There were no visits from his family. No letters or phone calls telling him how they missed him. There had been many lonely nights during his first years in the non-Amish world when he'd almost gone back.

Only having the eighth-grade education the Amish allowed made it tough finding a job. It had been tougher still getting a driver's license and a social security card, worldly things the Amish rejected. If it hadn't been for his dream of learning to fly, he might have gone back.

If Rebecca had been waiting for him, he would have gone back.

He hadn't planned to speak to her today. His only intention had been to come, buy her quilt to help her raise money for her surgery and then leave town. He had the best of intentions—right up to the moment she sat down in front of him.

So close he could have reached out and touched her. So close and yet so far.

His hands ached with the need to feel her fingers

entwined with his, the way they used to be when they had walked barefoot down a shady summer lane after the youth singings or a softball game. Life had been so simple then. It was so much more complicated now.

Why, after all this time, did she still have such a profound effect on him? Even from this distance he felt the pull of her presence the same way he felt the pull of the earth when he was flying above it.

He closed his eyes and shook his head. This was ridiculous. He wasn't some green farm boy enchanted by a pretty face. He was a sensible, grown man long past teenage infatuations. It had to be a combination of the flu and nostalgia brought on by being surrounded by people who shared the heritage he'd grown up with.

Everywhere he looked he saw Amish men with their beards and black felt hats. The women, wearing long dresses in muted solid colors with their white bonnets reminded him of his mother and his sisters.

Shy, solemn and subdued when among the English, the Amish were gentle, loving people, happy to quietly raise their families and continue in a life that seemed centuries out of touch with the modern world.

Would he even recognize his little brothers and sisters if they were here? Joseph, his baby brother, had been six when Gideon left. He'd be a teenager now and ready to begin his rumspringa. He would be free to explore worldly ways in order to understand what he was giving up before he took the vows of the faithful.

Did Joseph long for the outside world that had taken his older brother? If so, Gideon prayed he would go before his baptism. That way he could be free to visit his parents and see his old friends without being shunned. Gideon wondered about them often, thought of driving out to see them, but having left under such a cloud, he believed a clean break was the best way. Was it? How could he ever be sure?

Gideon adjusted his aviator sunglasses and glanced around. He doubted anyone he knew would recognize him. He wore a knit cap pulled low on his forehead. His hair was shaggy and a bit unkempt, unlike the uniformly neat haircuts of the Amish men around him.

His eyes were sunken and red from his illness and the long road trip. Two days' worth of beard stubble shadowed his cheeks. Glances in his rearview mirror on the way down showed a man who looked like death warmed over. No, no one was likely to recognize him. That was a good thing.

He was an English stranger, not the Amish youth who once asked Rebecca Beachy for her hand in marriage. Confusion swirled through his mind when he thought again of how she had deceived him.

He'd known her since their school days. They'd grown up on neighboring farms. They had courted for two full years and he proposed to her a week before her twenty-first birthday. Yet she'd just told him she learned she was going blind when she was twenty. Why hadn't she told him back then?

She broke his heart when she said she'd been mistaken about her feelings for him. Was that the truth or had it been a lie? Her sudden change of heart hadn't made sense back then any more than it did now.

Did she think he couldn't handle the truth? Or had she known he would eventually leave the Amish and tried to protect herself from that heartache? Maybe she'd wanted to spare him a lifetime spent with a blind wife.

Shouldn't that have been his choice to make?

His fingers curled into fists. Had he known the truth he would have stood by her.

Wouldn't he? Gideon bit the corner of his lip. Would knowing her condition have changed him from a dissatisfied youth itching to leave the restrictive Amish life into one who welcomed the challenge God placed before him?

He knew Rebecca wouldn't leave the faith. They'd had plenty of discussions about it in the months they were together. She knew of his discontent. When she broke off their courtship, he left home in a fit of sullen temper and cut himself off from everything and everyone he'd known. Because of her.

No, that wasn't fair. He left because he wanted something only the outside world could offer. He wanted to fly. He'd wanted her more, but without her his choice had been clear.

Would he have married Rebecca knowing she wouldn't be able to see his face or the faces of their children? He wanted to believe he would have, but he was far from sure.

He watched as several Amish women stopped to speak to her and the woman she sat with. One of them held a baby in her arms while a fussy toddler clung to her skirt. They were the same women he'd seen with her on television. The young mother handed her baby to Rebecca and picked up her older child, a little girl with dark hair and eyes.

Seeing a babe in Rebecca's arms reminded him of all she had missed in her life. Was it her choice never to marry? How strong she must be to face her hardship alone.

What was the cause of her blindness? Was it some inherited disease she didn't want to pass on to her children?

The Amish accepted handicapped children as special blessings from God. If she chose not to marry for that reason, then she wasn't being true to her faith any more than he had been.

Gideon pulled his knit cap lower over his brow.

Nothing about the past could be changed. It was pointless to wonder what would have happened if he'd stayed in their Amish community. He'd left that life long, long ago. It was closed to him now.

The past couldn't be changed but he could help shape a better future for Rebecca. He was here to raise money for her, not to reminisce about unrequited love. As the bidding began on her quilt, he raised his hand knowing it didn't matter what the quilt cost. He wasn't going home without it.

Rebecca couldn't believe her ears when a bidding war erupted over her quilt. With each jump in price shouted by the auctioneer she thought it couldn't possibly go higher, but it did. Higher and higher still.

Who could possibly want to pay so much for a quilt stitched by a blind woman? She grasped her aunt's arm. "Can you see the bidders?"

"*Ja.* It is between an *Englisch* fellow and Daniel Hershberger."

"Daniel is bidding on my quilt?"

Her aunt chuckled. "I told you the man was sweet on you."

The owner of a local mill that employed more than fifty people, Daniel was a well-respected Amish businessman. Although he was several years older than she was, he often stopped by to visit with her and her aunt. Rebecca shook her head at her aunt's assumption. "I think you're the one who caught his fancy."

"He doesn't make sheep eyes at me when he's sitting on the porch swing."

"I have only your word for that. I'm blind. What is the *Englisch* fellow like?"

"It's hard to tell. He's standing at the back. He's wearing a knit cap and a short leather jacket. He has dark glasses on."

"Is he young or old?" Rebecca wished her aunt had paid attention to the stranger sitting behind them earlier. Was he the one offering a ridiculously high price for her handiwork?

"Not too young. He has a scruffy short beard that so many *Englisch* boys seem to like. He looks pasty, like he's been ill."

It must be Booker. Rebecca smiled in satisfaction but her delight quickly faded. Was he bidding because of the quality of her work or because he felt sorry for her? It shouldn't matter but it did. She didn't want his pity.

But if he wasn't doing it out of pity, then why?

A strange excitement settled in her midsection when she thought about his low, gravelly voice speaking quietly in her ear. There was something about him that made her want to know him better.

The auctioneer shouted, "Sold!"

As the room erupted in chatter and applause, Rebecca asked, "Who got it?"

"The *Englisch*."

Rebecca stood up. "I must go and thank him. Can you take me to him?"

"Let the crowd thin out a little. Everyone is hurrying to get gone because the weather is getting worse. Ester Zook said it was already starting to sleet when she came in."

Once Booker left the event Rebecca knew she'd never have the chance to speak with him again. "I don't want to miss him. Please, it's important to me."

"Very well. I see him heading toward the front where people are paying for their purchases."

Rebecca walked beside her aunt against the flow of people leaving the tent and wished Vera would move faster. What if he paid for her quilt and left before she had the chance to thank him? It was foolish, really, this pressing need to speak to him. She didn't understand it, nor did she examine her feelings too closely. He was an outsider and thus forbidden to her.

Before they had gone more than a few feet, she heard Daniel Hershberger's voice at her side. "I'm right sorry I couldn't buy your quilt, Rebecca. It was uncommonly pretty."

"It was, wasn't it?" Vera replied, pausing to speak with him, to Rebecca's dismay.

"I didn't get the quilt, but rest assured I have

donated what money I can to your cause. I've already given a check to Bishop Zook."

Tamping down her impatience, Rebecca recognized Dan's exceptional act of charity for the gift it was. "*Danki,* my friend. God will bless your generosity. If you will excuse us, I wish also to thank the man who outbid you for the quilt. Do you see him?"

"Ja," Daniel replied. "He is in line waiting to pay. Before you go, I wanted to ask both of you to supper this coming Sunday. Unless you have other plans? My sister is coming and she can cook a fine meal."

"We do not have other plans," Vera answered before Rebecca could come up with a workable excuse.

Daniel was a good man and a friend, but Rebecca couldn't bring herself to see him as anything else. If her aunt was right and he wished to court her, he was in for a letdown.

"Excellent. What time shall I expect you?" His delight was clear.

Rebecca waited impatiently for the two of them to work out the details. She wanted to find Booker and speak to him before he left Hope Springs for good.

She wanted to thank him, yes, but there was another reason. One she didn't understand. She felt *compelled* to speak with him again. It didn't make any sense but she had learned to follow her instincts when her sight failed her.

Vera and Daniel continued discussing his dinner invitation. Suddenly, Rebecca couldn't wait any longer. "If you'll excuse me, I must go."

She unfolded her cane and moved forward, swinging it side to side as she went. Vera caught up with her. "Rebecca, what is wrong with you? That was rude."

"I don't want to miss speaking to Mr. Booker. Do you see him? Where is he?"

"Straight ahead of you, but slow down before you trip."

The line Gideon stood in moved quickly toward a set of tables where he could collect his expensive new quilt. He hoped they'd take a personal check. The bidding had far exceeded the amount of cash in his pocket. If they wouldn't take his check, he'd have to use his credit card and hope it didn't put him over his limit. This venture was foolhardy and expensive, but he was glad he had come.

When he reached the table, he took off his glasses and hung them on his shirt pocket. "Do you accept personal checks?"

The man at the table looked up and Gideon's heart dropped when he recognized his cousin, Adam Troyer, beneath the wide-brimmed straw hat. He was ten years older and sported the beard of a married man, but there was no mistaking him. Gideon steeled his heart against the humiliation to come and prayed he wouldn't be recognized.

Adam's eyes grew round. "Gideon? Is that you?"

So much for remaining incognito.

Surging to his feet, Adam grabbed Gideon's hand and began pumping it in a hearty shake. "I can't believe my eyes. What's it been? Seven, eight years?"

"Ten," Gideon croaked.

"Too long. What's the matter with your voice? You sound terrible."

"Laryngitis. It sounds worse than it is."

"What are you doing here?" Adam finally released Gideon's hand.

"Buying a quilt."

"Which one?"

"The one made by Rebecca Beachy." Gideon handed over the yellow card with his number on it.

"So, you were the bidder! I didn't recognize you from across the room. There is a lot of speculation going on about you. This is the most any quilt has brought in the history of Hope Springs." Adam nodded toward the women folding and packing the quilts into boxes behind him. They were all glancing his way.

"If you don't mind, I'd rather not have everyone know who I am. Have you forgotten? I'm under the ban."

Adam's face grew pensive. "I had forgotten. Like you, I went out into the world for many years, but

God brought me home. We would welcome you back to the church with great joy, Gideon."

"I'm not here to rejoin the faith. I'm only here to help Rebecca. She and I were…close once."

"I remember. We all thought you'd marry."

"So did I, but life doesn't often turn out the way we plan."

"Many are the plans in a man's heart, but it is the Lord's purpose that prevails."

Gideon gave his cousin a wry smile. "I should know that one."

"It's from Proverbs."

"Guess you can tell I haven't been reading my Bible."

Adam's gaze softened. "It's never too late, Gideon."

Pulling out his checkbook, Gideon ignored his cousin's comment and wrote a check for the price of the quilt. "If Rebecca learns the money came from me, from an ex-Amish, she might not accept it. I don't want to make trouble for her."

"I understand. After this meeting I will not know you, but it sure is *goot* to see you. Where are you staying?"

"I'm not staying. I'm driving back to Rochester, New York, tonight."

"Rochester? *Nee,* you aren't driving that way. The sheriff just told us the interstate has been closed south of Akron due to the ice storm."

"You're joking." This was a complication Gideon hadn't foreseen. He should have paid more attention to the weather forecast before jumping in his car and driving three hundred and fifty miles.

"It's settled," Adam declared. "You're staying with us. My wife, Emma, and I run the Wadler Inn. You can't miss it. It's on Main Street at the edge of town. We're normally booked solid during the auction, but we've had a couple of cancellations."

Gideon glanced around to make sure no one was listening. He leaned closer. "I'm under the ban, cousin. You cannot offer me a place to stay. Just speaking to me could cause trouble for you."

"You let me worry about that. The bishop here is a good man and just. Unlike your old bishop in Berlin, he is not eager to condemn a man for his sins. He truly believes in forgiveness. Besides, it is my duty to pray for you and to give aid to those in need. You look like you're in need. Go to the inn when you leave here and tell the man at the front desk that I sent you. There is no need to mention that you are my wayward cousin."

"Thanks, Adam. I appreciate it. Is there anyone else who might recognize me?" Gideon slipped his sunglasses back on. He knew what Adam was risking by associating with him. He risked being shunned by members of his church. Gideon wouldn't stay if it meant trouble for Adam.

"Some of my family lives near here, but they did

not come today. I'm not sure they would know you. You are much changed."

Relieved, Gideon signed his check and left it lying on the table knowing Adam should not accept anything from his hand.

With a slight nod, Adam acknowledged Gideon's thoughtfulness.

Gideon caught sight of Rebecca and her aunt making their way through the crowd in his direction. Turning back to Adam, he said, "As soon as the roads are open I'm out of here."

Adam's face grew serious. "Life doesn't always work out as we plan."

"If Rebecca asks for my name, tell her I wish to remain anonymous."

"I can do that. It is good to see you, cousin. I have missed you. All your family has missed you."

"I've missed you, too. How are…how are my parents?"

"I had a letter from them just last week. They are well. Your brother Levi has a new son. That makes four boys for him now."

"Levi is married? Scrawny, shy Levi?" Gideon found it hard to believe his brother had four kids. He was only a year younger than Gideon.

"Betty and Susie, too. They each have a girl and a boy."

He had eight nieces, nephews and in-laws he'd

never met. How sad was that? "Grandchildren must make my mother happy."

"Not as happy as having you return."

Gideon swallowed back the lump that rose in his throat. "When you see them—"

He paused. Coming here had been a mistake. It opened up far too many painful memories. "Tell them I'm doing well."

Taking his box with the quilt packed inside, Gideon turned and made his way toward the exit. Ten feet short of the opening he heard her call his name.

"Booker, please wait!"

Keep walking. Pretend you don't hear her.

His feet slowed. He could give good advice to himself but he apparently couldn't follow it.

What would it hurt to speak to her one more time? After today he'd never see her again. Just this once more.

Turning around, he waited until she reached him. Her aunt hung back, a faint look of displeasure on her face. It wasn't seemly for Rebecca to seek out an *Englisch* fellow.

She moved toward him until her cane touched his feet. When she opened her mouth to speak, he forestalled her. "I know what you're going to say, Miss Beachy, but there is no need."

He couldn't take his eyes off her face. He memorized the fine arch of her brows, the soft smile that curved her lips. She wore a pair of dark, wire-rimmed spectacles, but he knew her eyes were sky blue. If this was the last time he saw her face he wanted to remember it until the day he died.

"There is always a need to show our gratitude for the kindness of others, Mr. Booker."

"Consider me thanked. I've got to get going." Any second now he was going to blurt out his identity and undo all of the good he'd accomplished.

He was keenly aware of Rebecca's aunt standing a few paces back. A burly man came out of the crowd and stood with her, a look of displeasure formed on his face, too. Gideon turned his back to them. It was possible they'd met but he wasn't sure.

This was nuts. He wanted to see Rebecca again. He'd done that. He wanted to help her and he had.

Mission accomplished. Walk away.

No, what he really wanted was an answer to why she stopped loving him. But that was an answer he was never going to get.

"Good luck with your surgery, Miss Beachy. I wish you every success." He turned away and walked out into the stinging cold sleet.

Chapter Three

Rebecca held on to her aunt's arm as they entered the lobby of the Wadler Inn. The instant she stepped inside the building she was surrounded by the smells of wood smoke, baking bread and roasting meat. She felt the heat and heard the crackling of burning logs in the inn's massive fireplace to her right.

The clatter of cutlery and plates being gathered together as tables were cleared came from her left. The Shoofly Pie Café was adjacent to the inn and accessible through a set of wide pocket doors. The murmur of voices and sounds told Rebecca the doors were open. The discordant noise increased the headache growing behind her eyes.

As her aunt moved forward, Rebecca automatically counted her steps so she could navigate the room by herself in the future. Although she had stayed at the inn several times in the past, she needed to refresh the layout in her mind. She thought she knew the place well, but a chair carelessly moved by one of the guests or a new piece of furniture could present unseen obstacles for her.

The thump of feet coming down the stairs and the whisper of a hand sliding over a banister told her the inn's open staircase was just ahead. The tick-tock of a grandfather clock beside the stairway marked its location for Rebecca.

"Velkumm." Emma Troyer's cheerful voice grew closer as she left the stairs and came toward them.

"Hello, Emma." Rebecca smiled in her direction.

"I just finished readying your room. I'm so happy you decided to stay with us again."

"We're glad to be here," Vera replied.

Staying at the inn had become a ritual for the two women following the quilt auctions. It was a time Vera truly enjoyed when the work of cooking, cleaning, sewing and running the farm was put on hold for a few days so she could relax and visit her many friends in town.

Rebecca would rather be back in her aunt's small house. The openness of the inn disoriented her, but she never said as much. Rebecca loved her aunt dearly. Vera deserved her little holiday each year. If Rebecca had insisted on staying home alone, her aunt would have cancelled her plans and come home, too.

Emma said, "Rebecca, I couldn't believe it when I heard how much your quilt went for."

"God was good to us," Vera said quickly.

Rebecca shook her head. "It was not worth that much money. The *Englisch* fellow who bought it did so out of pity. He saw a story about me on his television. That's the only reason he came."

Vera patted Rebecca's arm. "It matters not what his motivation was. His being there was God's doing."

"How much more money will you need for your surgery?" Emma asked.

"Another twenty thousand dollars," Vera answered.

"So much?" Emma's voice echoed the doubt in Rebecca's heart. It was unlikely they could raise enough money in time.

She said, "Doctor White has told us the surgeon who is perfecting this operation is moving to Sweden to open a special clinic there after Christmas. If we can't raise the rest of the money before then it will be too late."

Emma laid her hand on Rebecca's shoulder. "Do not give up hope. We know not what God has planned for our lives."

Rebecca swallowed the lump in her throat and nodded. "I must accept His will in this."

"Are you hungry?" Emma asked. "We've started serving supper in the café."

Vera said, “I could eat a horse.”

“*Goot.* My mother has been waiting impatiently for you. I’ll tell her you’re here and we can catch up on all the news. Did you hear my *Aenti* Wilma over in Sugarcreek broke her hip last week?”

Rebecca said, “You two go ahead. I think I would rather lie down for a while before I eat.”

“Is your headache worse?” Vera asked.

Rebecca appreciated her aunt’s concern. “*Nee.* I’m sure a few minutes of peace and quiet are all I need.”

“Let me show you to your room,” Emma offered.

“I can find my way,” Rebecca insisted. She didn’t want to be treated like an invalid.

“Very well. I’ve put you in number seven, the same as last year.” Emma pressed an old-fashioned key into Rebecca’s hand.

“*Danki.* Enjoy your visit.”

She opened the white folding cane she carried and headed toward the ticking clock she knew sat beside the staircase. The clock began to strike the hour. It was five o’clock.

When she located the first riser, she went up the steps slowly, holding tight to the banister. There were fifteen steps if she remembered correctly. When her searching toe found the top of the landing, she smiled. Fifteen it was.

She walked down the hallway, letting her cane sweep from side to side. The rooms were numbered with evens on the left and odds on the right. It took only a few moments to locate her door.

She fumbled with the key for a second and lost her grip on it. It fell, struck her toe and bounced away. The hallway was carpeted. She couldn't tell from the sound where the key landed.

Annoyed, Rebecca dropped to her knees and began searching with her hands, letting her fingers glide over the thick pile. The carpeting was a concession to the English guests that stayed at the inn. Amish homes held no such fanciness. A plain plank floor or simple linoleum was all anyone needed.

The sound of a door opening across the hall sent a rush of embarrassed heat to her cheeks. A second later the door closed.

She knew who it was. She recognized the spicy scent of his aftershave. Her heartbeat skittered and took off like a nervous colt at a wild gallop.

The silence stretched on until she thought she must have been mistaken. He didn't move, didn't speak. She cocked her head to the side. "Is someone there?"

"Can I help?" His raspy voice was a mere whisper.

It was Booker. God had given her another chance to spend time with him. "You have already helped a great deal. The price you paid for my quilt was outrageous."

"Some works of art are priceless, but what are you doing on the floor?"

"I dropped my room key."

"Ah. I see it." A second later he grasped her hand and pressed the cool metal key into her palm, then gently closed her fingers over it.

Waves of awareness raced up her arm and sent shivers dancing across her nerve endings. She didn't trust her voice to speak as he cupped her elbows and drew her to her feet. The warmth from his hands spread through her body, making it difficult to breathe.

She'd known this dizzying sensation only once before. The first and only time Gideon Troyer had kissed her. Would this man's kiss light up her soul the way Gideon's had?

Shame rushed in on the heels of her disgraceful thought. What was the matter with her? This man was *Englisch*. He was forbidden, and she was foolish to place herself in such a situation.

She was inches away from him. Gideon's pulse pounded in his ears like a drum as he studied Rebecca's face, her lips, the curve of her cheek. Behind her tinted glasses he saw the way her full lashes lay dark and smoky against her fair skin. The long ribbons of her white *kapp* drew his attention to the faint pulse beating at the side of her neck just where he wanted to press a kiss.

She was everything he remembered and so much more. The girl he once loved had matured into a beautiful woman. He longed to pull her into his arms and kiss her. To see if those lush lips tasted as sweet as they did in his memory.

His grip tightened. Suddenly, she grew tense in his grasp and tried to pull away.

He was frightening her. This wasn't a romantic interlude from their past for her. To her he was a stranger. He released her, took a step back and tried to put her at ease. "Would you like me to open the door for you?"

"No. I can manage." She retreated until her back was against the wood.

She didn't look frightened, only flustered. A pretty blush added color to her cheeks. Adam must have known she was staying at the inn. It would have helped if his cousin had given him a heads-up.

Gideon said, "It was nice talking to you. Perhaps we'll see each other later since the ice is going to keep me here for a day. Wait, should I use the word *see,* or is that being insensitive?"

"I beg your pardon?" Her flustered look changed to confusion.

"I don't know how to address a blind person. You're the first one I've met. Can you give me a few pointers so I don't stick my foot in my mouth?"

Her charming smile twitched at the corner of her mouth. "There isn't a special way to address us, and you don't have to be concerned about using the word *see.* I use it all the time."

"Good, because I'm thinking it would be hard to have a conversation with you if I constantly had to think up a way to replace every word that relates to sight."

She nodded slowly. "I see what you mean."

"Right!"

Chuckling, she said, "I'm sure we'll run into each other if you're staying here for a while. The inn isn't very big."

"I'd call it cozy."

"I don't find it so."

"Why not?" Was she uncomfortable because he was here?

She shrugged. "It's not important."

"Of course it is."

Following a moment of hesitation, she said, "I feel lost when I'm downstairs. The ceiling is so high that sounds echo differently. It's that way in this long hall, too. I'm used to my aunt's small farmhouse. I know where everything is. I can move about freely."

"You're comfortable there."

She smiled. "That's right. You do *see* what I mean."

"If you need help navigating your way around, just ask me."

Her smile faded. "I'm not asking for your help. I can manage quite well on my own."

"Ouch. The lady is touchy."

Her mouth dropped open in surprise. "I am not."

"Could have fooled me. That's not very Amish of you."

Her mouth snapped shut. "What is that supposed to mean?"

"The Amish are humble folks. Humble people accept help when it's offered."

Torn between scolding him and turning the other cheek, as she knew she should, Rebecca pressed her lips closed on her comment. He was baiting her. She didn't have to respond.

"I'm right. Let me hear you admit it."

She said, "The Amish strive to be humble before God."

"Gets hard to do sometimes, doesn't it?"

She blew out a long breath. "Yes, sometimes it is hard. Anything worthwhile is often hard to obtain. That is why we must depend on God to aid us."

"Sorry if I offended you."

"You did, but you are forgiven. My aunt often tells me I am too proud and I must seek humility."

"It's a foolish person who doesn't heed *goot* advice."

Hearing her own words tossed back at her made Rebecca smile. "I do need to work on that."

Downstairs she heard the grandfather clock chiming the quarter hour and realized her headache had disappeared. Conversing with Booker was interesting to say the least. No one had ever asked if talking about her blindness made her uncomfortable. Usually they stammered apologies or sought to avoid mentioning it all together.

"What kind of work do you do?" she asked.

"I own a small airplane charter service."

"You are a pilot?"

"Yes."

Sadness settled over her. "I once knew a young Amish man who wanted to fly. Is it wonderful to soar above the earth like a bird?"

"It has its moments. What happened to him?"

She grasped the key so tightly her fingers ached and she fought back tears. "The lure of the world pulled him away from our faith and he never came back."

After a long pause, he asked, "Were the two of you close?"

"*Ja,* very close." Why was she sharing this with a stranger? Perhaps, because in some odd way he reminded her of Gideon.

"Did you ever think about going with him?"

She smiled sadly. "I didn't believe he would leave. For a long time I thought it was my fault, but I know now it was not."

Booker stepped closer. "How can you be so sure?"

She raised her chin. "He vowed before God and the people of our church to live by the rules of our Amish faith. If he could turn his back on his vow to God, it was not because of me."

"I imagine you're right about that. Have you forgiven him?"

She wished she could hear him speak in his normal voice. It was hard to read his emotions in the forced whisper he had to use. "Of course."

"If he came back, what would you do?"

"If he came to ask forgiveness and repent I would be happy for him and for his family. I can have Emma Troyer make you some blackcurrant tea. It will make your throat better in no time."

"That's what my mother used to do."

Did she imagine it or did she hear sorrow in his voice? "Is something wrong?"

"I haven't seen my mother in many years."

"Why?"

"I'm estranged from my family."

"That is a very sad thing. Only God is more important than our families. You should go visit them as soon as you can. Thanksgiving is coming in a few weeks. That, surely, is reason enough to put aside your pride and go home."

"I wish that were possible, but it's not. Good day, Rebecca."

She didn't want him to leave but she couldn't think of a way to stop him. The carpet muffled his footsteps as he walked away. She waited until she heard him descending the stairs before she entered her room.

She closed the door and leaned against it. What

did he look like? Was he handsome or plain? What made him sad when he talked about his family? Why hadn't he visited them? There were many things she wanted to know about Booker.

And curiosity killed the cat.

The old adage popped into her mind like the warning it was meant to be. She knew full well it was dangerous to become involved with an outsider. Yet there was something familiar about him that nagged at the back of her mind. Something that made her believe they'd met before. If that were true, why wouldn't he simply say so?

Booker was a riddle. A riddle she wanted to solve. The thought of being cooped up at the inn suddenly took on a whole new outlook. He would be here, too.

Chapter Four

After leaving Rebecca, Gideon descended the stairs of the inn and headed for the café. For the first time in three days he had an appetite. He entered the dining area and was seated by a young Amish waitress.

He accepted an offer of coffee while he studied the menu. After the waitress filled a white mug and set it before him, he added a splash of real cream from a small pewter pitcher on the table. He took a cautious sip of the hot rich blend. Even though his voice hadn't returned, swallowing wasn't as painful. A second sip of coffee went down as smoothly as the first. Maybe he was finally on the mend.

Pulling his cell phone from his pocket he clicked the weather app and checked the local weather and road closings again. The storm that had coated the northern half of the state in ice was gearing up to add a foot or more of snow to the rest of the state.

He wasn't going home tonight, but it was unlikely the roads would be closed for long. Once the storm passed, he'd be on his way. If not first thing in the morning, at least by the afternoon. He sent a text message to Roseanne notifying her that he wouldn't be in to the office in the morning.

Her reply was succinct. *Good!*

Gideon closed his phone and turned his attention to the people around him. The café's customers were mostly Amish enjoying a special treat of eating out after the auction. He remembered many times like this with his family. Although his mother professed to be annoyed with the expense, everyone knew she secretly enjoyed not having to cook.

There were a few non-Amish present in the café, too. He was the only one dining alone. Everyone else sat with family or friends.

His gaze was drawn to an Amish father, a man about his own age, seated with four small children and his wife at the table across the aisle. When their food arrived, the man took his infant son's hands and held them between his own as he bowed his head in prayer. The baby protested only briefly before keeping still. Children were expected to behave and quickly learned the value of copying their elders.

Gideon knew the prayer the man was silently reciting. It was the *Gebet Nach Dem Essen,* the Prayer Before Meals.

O Lord God, heavenly Father, bless us and these thy gifts, which we accept from thy tender goodness. Give us food and drink also for our souls unto life eternal, that we may share at thy heavenly table, through Jesus Christ. Amen.

The Lord's Prayer, also prayed silently, would follow the prayer before meals as well as the prayer after meals. Gideon hadn't prayed much since he left home. A sense of shame crept over him. He had plenty to be grateful for and no good reason to ignore the blessings he'd received.

The Amish father lifted his head, signaling the end of the prayer for everyone at the table. He patted his son's golden curls and began cutting up the meat on the boy's plate. It was a simple act, but it moved Gideon to wonder if he would ever do the same with children of his own.

Maybe it was time he settled down and started looking around for a woman to spend his life with. He hadn't already because the business took up all of his time. He'd been so intent on making a place for himself in the English world that he'd failed to notice the place he made was hollow and empty of love.

He had few friends other than Craig. He lived in a sterile one-bedroom apartment, ate takeout in front of his flat-screen TV. He had neighbors he barely knew and rarely saw. He'd avoided going to church in spite of Roseanne's occasional urging and invitations. It wasn't much of a life when he looked at it that way. Except for the flying. When he was in the clouds he was happy.

He closed his eyes. The smell of baking bread and pot roast filled the air. He thought back to the food his mother used to make. Roast beef and pork, fried chicken, schnitzel with sauerkraut, served piping hot from her wood-burning stove with fresh bread and vegetables from her garden.

As a kid, he never gave a thought to how much work his mother did without complaint. All he'd thought about was escaping the narrow, inflexible Amish way of life. Had it really been so bad?

I must be sick if I'm longing for the good old days.

He sat up and motioned the waitress over. Before he could place his order, the outside door opened and his cousin Adam walked in. Their eyes met for a long second. Adam looked away first. He walked past Gideon without so much as a nod of recognition. Gideon didn't expect the snub to hurt as much as it did.

Adam was being true to his faith. It was his duty to shun a wayward member, to remind Gideon he had cut himself off from God as well as from his family. Gideon had known for years that he would be shunned if he returned unrepentant, but he had never experienced the treatment firsthand.

Years ago, his mother explained to him that shunning was done out of love, to show people the error of their ways, not to punish them. It didn't feel that way at the moment. Gideon's newfound appetite deserted him.

Adam stepped behind the counter and took over the cash register. The waitress beside Gideon's table asked, "Have you decided what you'd like?"

"What kind of soup do you have?"

Her eyebrows shot up in surprise at his hoarse whisper. "We've got homemade chicken noodle soup today. I'll bring you a bowl. You sound like you need it," she said with a sympathetic smile.

He folded the menu and tucked it between the sugar jar and the ketchup bottle. "That'll be fine."

His soup arrived at the same moment Rebecca walked in.

She stood poised in the doorway to the inn with her cane in hand. She tilted her head slightly, as if concentrating on the sounds of the room. A smile lit her face and she moved ahead to a booth by the window. It was then he saw her aunt seated with several older Amish women. They greeted Rebecca warmly and made room for her to sit with them.

He was impressed that she had been able to pick out her aunt's voice in the crowded room and locate her without assistance. She moved with a confidence he admired. If being at the inn made her uncomfortable it didn't show at the moment.

Gideon slowly stirred his soup and unobtrusively watched her.

* * *

Was he in the room?

Rebecca wished she could ask her aunt or her friends if Booker was in the café. She didn't, because she knew it would seem odd. The last thing she wanted was to draw attention to her preoccupation with him.

It was bad enough that she *had* this preoccupation with a total stranger. She didn't need to share her foolishness with anyone else.

"Nettie, how are Katie and Elam these days?" Vera asked.

"My boy is over the moon with his new *sohn.* Katie is a fine *mudder* and a strong woman. Little Rachel doesn't quite know what to make of her new *bruder.* She is used to being the apple of her *daed's* eye, you know."

Emma said, "I have some news that I have been dying to share."

When she didn't say anything else, Nettie prompted, "Well, what is it?"

"Adam and I are expecting." Her voice brimmed with barely contained excitement.

"Congratulations. That's *wunderbaar.*" Rebecca was truly delighted to hear that her friends were to become parents.

Vera echoed Rebecca's congratulations and said, "To think you were considered an old maid until a year ago."

Naomi, Emma's mother, chuckled. "When Adam moved to town, right away he saw my Emma for the good woman she truly is. It just goes to show God has His plans for each of us in His own time."

"That He does," Emma agreed. "Adam and I are going to visit his family and share the news tomorrow. If the weather cooperates."

Vera grasped Rebecca's arm. "We must make a quilt for this new blessing."

Rebecca agreed. "*Ja,* we will."

She toyed with her food as her companions talked about babies, the weather and the turnout for the auction. She had made quilts for all the babies of her friends and family, but there were no quilts for children of her own.

She had turned aside every romantic overture that had come her way. There had been a few over the years, but not many. In Hope Springs, the single women outnumbered the men for it was usually the young men who were lured away by the outside world. Why would a man who remained choose a blind woman for a wife when he had healthy ones to pick from?

Besides, none of the men had been Gideon. It was hard to imagine giving her heart to anyone else.

Why? What was she waiting for? Was she hoping Gideon would come back and declare his love again? She had turned down his offer of marriage because she loved him. Because she believed he deserved better than a blind millstone around his neck. Fear and the painful knowledge that she didn't deserve such happiness made her turn away from him.

If she could undo anything in her life, she would change only one thing—the night she slipped away with her sister Grace to join Gideon and his friends at a forbidden party. That one night changed everything.

She shut out the memory. Gideon wasn't coming back, and she had nothing to show for her sacrifice. One day she would be old and alone, without even her aunt to care for. What would happen to her then? She could go back to her parents, but when they were gone, which of her brothers or sisters would she go to live with? Any of them would take her in, but would they do so with joy in their hearts? It was unlikely.

Would it be so bad to marry Daniel Hershberger? If she did, she would have a house of her own and the hope of children. She might learn to love him in time. Daniel was a good man.

If only the thought of kissing him didn't leave her cold.

When their supper was finished, Rebecca went back to her room and sat alone on the bed. Her aunt had gone to her friend Naomi's home for a comfortable evening of visiting. Rebecca had been invited, but used her headache as an excuse not to go. In the silence of her room, Rebecca found herself thinking again about Booker.

How was he feeling? Was he sitting alone in his room as she was? Was he thinking about her? It warmed her to think she might be on his mind.

He was an intriguing man. Perhaps it was just his pitiful voice that made him so. When he could speak plainly, she might find him dull. Or not. She couldn't get him out of her head.

He'd said he wasn't married, and she had to wonder why.

Which was a silly thing to be thinking about!

In a fit of disgust, she got up and took out her Christmas Star quilt. She had only the binding to finish. It wouldn't take long. Perhaps if her hands were busy, her mind wouldn't wander into forbidden territory.

Early the next morning, Gideon walked out the inn's front door and entered a world frozen and cocooned in white. Snowflakes continued to fall, settling soundlessly onto the sidewalk behind a shopkeeper who had just cleared a path from his doorway to the street. Tree branches bent low beneath the weight of their white frosting. Everywhere, a hushed silence engulfed the town.

A few hardy souls had already ventured out. Directly across the street, a man worked to uncover his car with an ice scraper that was clearly too small for the job.

The quiet gave way to the jingle of harness bells. As they grew louder, Gideon looked down the street to see a horse-drawn sleigh coming his way. An Amish family with six rosy-cheeked children filling the back of the sleigh drove past him. Their eyes were bright with the excitement of the ride.

The man digging out his car met Gideon's gaze and grinned. "I've got one hundred and fifty horses under the hood for all the good they are doing me at the moment while the Amish go flying by with only one horse. I reckon the simple life has some advantages, after all."

Gideon grinned as he stood in front of the inn with no particular destination in mind. He just wanted to be out. Out in the clean fresh air of a snow-covered small Ohio town. Hope Springs was a lot like Berlin. A little bigger, but not by much. The same type of stores crowded together off the tree-lined streets.

He noticed antiques for sale and a touristy Amish gift shop down the street. The merchandise there likely came from China and not from the local craftsmen. Across the street was a hardware store. A pharmacy sat sandwiched between the hardware store and a clothing store. A little farther on a gas station sat at the corner.

Hope Springs wasn't that different from a hundred other Ohio towns. Oddly, after ten years in the city, Gideon felt right at home on these streets. Time to explore a little. Left or right?

Before he made up his mind he heard the door of the inn open behind him. To his surprise, Rebecca came out. She was bundled up against the cold in a heavy, dark blue woolen coat. A black bonnet covered her head. In one hand she clutched her purse. In the other hand she held her white cane. With little hesitation, she turned left and began walking down the sidewalk swinging her cane lightly in front of her.

He should have spoken, but he wasn't sure how his voice would sound this morning. What if she recognized him when he spoke?

Gideon followed her and watched as she tested the height and depth of a snowdrift in her path at the corner. She wasn't really going to try and find her way around town in these conditions, was she? Where was her aunt? Why wasn't someone with her?

To his astonishment, she made her way over the snowdrift easily and continued across the icy street. It was then he saw an obstacle she couldn't detect with her cane. There was no way for her to know the snow-laden branches of the trees that lined the avenue were hanging at shoulder level. She was about to walk into a cold surprise. He tried calling out a warning but his voice failed him.

Galvanized into action, Gideon hurried after her. He raced across the slick street as fast as he dared. Rebecca would get a face full of snow in another few steps. He tried again to call out. This time he managed to croak, "Rebecca, stop."

She paused and turned her head as if searching for the source of the pitiful sound he'd made. He reached the curb but hit a patch of ice on the sidewalk. His feet flew out from under him and he landed with a painful thud at Rebecca's feet.

He moaned and rubbed the back of his smarting head. When he opened his eyes, she was standing over him, her face silhouetted against the cloudy winter sky. He knew from memory that her eyes were the blue of a bright summer's day but she held them closed now behind her dark glasses.

He wanted her to open her eyes so he could see them. He wanted to see all the memories they held of their time together.

He wanted her to see him.

Two words, his name, would be all it would take to let her know who he was. If he said those two words would she turn away? Would she shun him? He couldn't take that risk.

"Are you all right?" She located him with her cane and bent down to assist him.

He gave a groan as he managed to leverage himself to sitting position. "I think so," he whispered.

"Booker?"

"Yes."

She slipped her hand beneath his elbow. "You poor man. Let me help you."

"Thanks." He accepted her assistance as he rose to his feet and dusted the snow from his clothes.

"Are you sure you aren't hurt?"

"I've got a pretty hard head."

"You shouldn't rush on these slippery walks. What were you thinking? Where were you going in such a hurry?"

It wasn't the first time he'd been chided for his lack of common sense by this woman. He'd missed her occasional scolding as much as he'd missed her tenderhcarted sweetness.

"I was hurrying to save you from walking into some snow-laden branches hanging over the walkway."

Her frown changed to the smile he adored. "Bless you for your concern, Booker. I would not enjoy getting a face full of snow."

"I didn't think you would."

"Now that I have been warned, I will be fine. Thank you for your concern."

"Where are you off to on such a cold day?"

"To the fabric shop."

"I was going that way. Do you mind if I walk along with you?"

She arched one eyebrow. "You are going to the fabric shop?"

"I didn't say I was going to the fabric shop. I said I was going that way. Two different things. If you would rather walk alone I understand."

She shook her head and started walking. "I don't mind the company, but you must promise not to continually try to help me."

"Why shouldn't I offer my help?"

She swung the cane from side to side, tapped it briefly on the sidewalk in front of her. "Because unless I ask for it, I don't really need it."

"All right, but three steps ahead of you are those low branches."

She moved closer to the building. "Am I clear if I walk over here?"

"Yeah. Are there any other rules I should know?" For a few words his voice came out strong and normal before breaking again. He froze, wondering if she would recognize him now.

"You should not grab a blind person. It's rude. You should not shout at someone who is blind because most of us can hear quite well."

"Can I ask questions or is that rude, too?" He kept his voice to a whisper. It might be best to stay silent but he didn't want to give up this opportunity to spend time with her.

"Questions are okay."

"Is it true that your hearing becomes more acute?"

"No. A blind person's hearing does not change. We simply pay more attention to what we hear."

He glanced down the walkway ahead of them. "I guess that makes sense. How will you know when you have reached the fabric shop?"

"Because I have been here many times." She stopped in front of a store called Needles and Pins.

"You counted your steps."

"I often do, but that's hard when I'm carrying on a conversation."

"I don't understand how you did it, then."

"The answer is right under your feet." She tapped the sidewalk through the layer of snow that hadn't yet been removed.

"I still don't get it."

"Listen." She took a step back and tapped again.

He listened intently, wanting to learn all that she was willing to teach. She stepped forward and tapped twice more. This time he heard the difference in the sound. Crouching down, he swept the snow aside. "It's brick, not concrete."

Her smile was bright and genuine. "*Ja.* Very *goot.* The store has a decorative brick design on the sidewalk in front of it. It makes it easy to find. Thank you for your escort, Booker."

"My pleasure," he whispered.

She hesitated, then pulled open the door and went inside.

Warmth and the scent of new fabrics surrounded Rebecca as she entered Needles and Pins, but her thoughts stayed with the man outside. His thoughtfulness pleased her. His consideration might be motivated by pity but she didn't think so. His kindness made her feel special. Made her feel feminine, something she hadn't experienced in the company of a man for many years.

"Hello, Rebecca. I've been expecting you."

Rebecca brushed aside her thoughts about Booker and turned to smile at Sarah Wyse, an Amish widow who worked at the shop. Rebecca wished her good morning in Pennsylvania Dutch. "*Guder mariye,* Sarah. How are you?"

"I'm fine. Everyone is talking about how well your quilt did yesterday. We are so pleased God has smiled on your efforts."

"*Danki.* Has my aunt's order come in?"

"*Ja,* yesterday morning. I'll get it for you."

Rebecca heard Sarah walk away. A few minutes later she returned. A muffled thud told Rebecca she had placed a large bolt of material on the wooden countertop.

"This is the lot I was telling your aunt about. It's a soft shade of lavender and we got an excellent buy on a large quantity."

Reaching out, Rebecca fingered the fabric. It was a cotton-polyester blend that would be durable enough for everyday dresses. "You are sure it is a color the bishop will find acceptable?"

"I hope so. His wife ordered six yards of it."

"We'll take it, then. I'll also take any of the fabric remnants you have."

"I bundled some together for you last night. Tell your aunt she can send back anything that doesn't work."

"Danki."

When Sarah rang up the total, Rebecca drew out her wallet and carefully searched through the folded bills. With her aunt's help, Rebecca was able to separate the identical-feeling currency. The ones folded lengthwise were one-dollar bills, those folded in half were ten-dollar bills and the ones folded in thirds were twenty-dollar bills.

Sarah handed back Rebecca's change and asked, "Who is your friend outside? Wouldn't he like to come in out of the cold?"

"He's waiting outside?"

"He's leaning against the lamppost and beginning to look like an icicle."

"Excuse me a moment." Rebecca turned and made her way to the door. Pulling it open, she called out, "Booker, what do you think you're doing?"

Chapter Five

"Are you trying to catch pneumonia?" Rebecca demanded.

For a long moment Booker didn't answer. Then she heard the crunch of his footsteps approaching through the snow. "How did you know I was waiting?"

"I heard your teeth chattering." She stepped back to allow him inside.

"You couldn't hear that, could you? Man, it feels good in here."

"I can hear them now. You don't have the sense God gave a goose."

"I'm not sure that's true."

"Why are you waiting outside?" she demanded.

"To walk you back to the inn."

"I thought you had somewhere to go."

"Not really."

Exasperated, she said, "I'm perfectly capable of finding my way back unaided."

"I believe you."

His voice was so hoarse she wanted to wrap him up in warm flannel and poor hot tea into him. "If you know I can find my way back then why were you waiting for me?"

"I enjoy spending time with you."

And she enjoyed spending time with him. This had to stop. "Booker, you barely know me."

"That can change."

She crossed her arms and tried to look stern. "Is this concern because I'm blind?"

"No. Why would you think that?"

From behind her, Rebecca heard Sarah ask, "Is everything all right?"

"*Ja,* everything is fine," Rebecca answered.

She spoke softly to Booker. "You should go back to the inn."

"I'm not in a rush. Besides, it's toasty warm in here. This may be a dumb question, but how do you choose the fabrics for your quilts?"

Rebecca heard the outside door open. A gust of cold air carried in the sounds of several Amish women speaking in Pennsylvania Dutch. The more people who saw her with Booker the more likely it was that she would become the object of gossip. It was time to end this…whatever it was.

"I must be going." She started toward the door and hurried outside. A second later, she heard someone come out behind her. If it was Booker, it would be best to ignore him. She made her way down the sidewalk. Footsteps told her someone was walking beside her.

After a dozen steps, Booker asked, "So how do you do it? How do you know what fabrics to use?"

"Why do you want to know?"

"Because you are an interesting person, and I admire your skill."

He was as tenacious as a toothache. Other than ordering him away, she couldn't see how to rid herself of his company.

She sighed heavily. "My aunt and I work together. We decide on a pattern, she picks the fabrics. You may have noticed that her hands are crippled. The women from our church district do the cutting for us. My aunt separates the pieces by color and I stitch them together. When the piecing is done, the quilt goes into a frame and I quilt the front and back together."

"I figured it had to be something like that. Don't you prick your fingers while you're trying to sew?"

She stopped in frustration. "Very rarely. What are you doing?"

"I'm going back to the inn like you told me to do. Is there somewhere else you'd like me to go? You can tell me."

She struggled not to smile and lost the battle. "I'm not going to the inn. It's the other way."

"Then I'm lost. I'll have to stick with you until

you can lead me home. Can we get moving? This cold wind is very bad for my throat."

"You should've thought of that before you left the warm, cozy inn," she countered, but started walking anyway.

"I hate being cooped up inside. I'm not used to it. I needed to get out for a while. I've been grounded for days now."

"What does that mean?"

"I haven't been able to fly."

It clearly bothered him. "Flying is important to you?"

"Very. It's my job."

Gideon had talked endlessly about wanting to fly. Some part of her needed to understand why. They turned a corner. The building blocked the wind giving them shelter and a sense of elusive warmth. Rebecca stopped. "What's it like to fly?"

There was a long moment of silence, then he said, "How can I describe it? It's freedom. I've been inside the clouds. I've looked down on mountaintops. Fields and farms below look like one of your quilts. I've seen the backs of birds flying beneath me, and I understand what makes them sing. To be suspended between heaven and earth is like no other feeling. It's…freedom."

"Walking upon the earth God has made is not joy enough?"

"It never has been for me."

She shook her head. "I don't think I understand."

He stepped closer. "I think you do. Because even though you can hear the birds sing you would give anything to see them winging their way across an expanse of bright blue sky. We can't control what we feel. Some things make us happy. Other things make us sad. You're sad right now."

How could this stranger see so deeply into her heart? "Maybe I am."

"You said you learned you were going blind when you were twenty. What caused it?"

"A simple, innocent thing."

"Tell me about it."

"Someone threw a snowball that had a sliver of a pine needle in it. It struck me in the eye."

She heard Booker suck in his breath and rushed to reassure him it was an accident. "My friend had no intention of hurting me. We were having fun. He took me straight to the doctor as soon as he realized what had happened. The doctor removed the sliver from my eye and we thought everything was fine."

"But you weren't fine."

"No. A few months later, I noticed the color of things starting to fade away. I went back to the doctor. His nurse drove me to see a specialist. There, I learned that I had a rare form of a disease called uveitis. There was little that could be done for me. I was told I would go completely blind within a year or two."

After a long pause of silence, Booker said, "Your friend, he must have felt terrible."

"I never told him."

"Why not?"

"My blindness is God's will, Booker. Why should I burden the heart of a friend with the knowledge that he was the instrument God chose?"

"Maybe because he had the right to know."

She struggled against the lump forming at the back of her throat. "He gave up that right."

"Why do you say that?

"He left the Amish. If his faith had been stronger, I might have told him, but he was gone before I could gather my courage."

"If you'd told him the truth, perhaps his faith would have been strong enough."

Didn't she wonder that very thing? No, Gideon had made his choice of his own free will.

"It's in the past. It can't be changed." She started walking again. She didn't care if Booker followed or not.

Gideon remembered the day it happened. It had been a snowy day much like today. Their friends, a dozen teenagers, had all gathered together for a skating party on his family's farm pond. He wasn't sure who threw the first snowball, but everyone joined in the free-for-all.

He could still see Rebecca, laughing as she

scooped up a handful to chuck his way. He ducked around a little pine tree, the only available cover. He knew she had a good aim. When her shot splattered against the tree trunk, he grabbed a handful of snow, packed it tight and hurled one back at her. His aim had been dead-on. It hit her square in the face. He'd laughed like crazy until he saw she was hurt.

His foolish act had caused her blindness. No wonder she had turned down his offer of marriage.

But it had been an accident. He never meant to hurt her. Never meant to hurt anyone. In the buggy on the way to the doctor he begged her forgiveness. She gave it freely. He clung to that thought. She forgave him for the injury, but she clearly hadn't forgiven him for leaving the faith.

He followed and caught up with her as she crossed the next street. It was time to tell her who he was.

And then what?

Would she insist on returning his money? If he wouldn't take it she might give it away. She was stubborn to a fault. Would his confession jeopardize her only chance at regaining her sight?

"I know you are following me, Booker."

He couldn't risk telling her the truth. "I can't leave while you're giving me such a wonderful tour of the town."

"I believe your voice is sounding stronger."

He whispered, "It comes and goes. Where to next?"

"The harness shop."

"It's got to be more interesting than the fabric store."

She chuckled. "*Ja,* for you, maybe."

Turning aside without warning, Rebecca entered a narrow alley. Overhead, large icicles had formed along the roof edges of the buildings. In the center of the alley the snow was deep. She stumbled, and Gideon took her arm. "Careful. If I lose you I'll never find my way back to the inn. I can see the headlines now. Frozen Tourist Turned into Tall Popsicle."

"Are you *ever* serious?"

"If you could see my face you'd know I'm dead serious."

She flashed a smile that warmed him down to his toes. "I doubt that."

They came out of the alley into a clearing where several buggies sat waiting for repairs. They made their way between the vehicles and up to the back door of a wooden building. She didn't bother knocking. Instead, she opened the door and went inside.

Gideon followed her into the cavernous interior where every type of harness and tack were hanging from the walls, the ceiling and display racks. A large propane-powered sewing machine sat in the center of the room by an enormous cutting table.

Along one wall, an ancient workbench held dozens of awls and leatherworking tools, all arranged neatly in holders. Near the front of the store, a coal-burning stove added warmth to the large space.

Rebecca called out, "*Daadi,* are you here?"

"What is this? Has my favorite grandchild come to visit at last?" A small bandy-legged Amish elder came from the front of the store.

His snow-white hair held a permanent crease from the hat he normally wore. His beard, as white as his hair, reached the center of the dark vest buttoned over his pale blue shirt. His sharp eyes looked Gideon up and down in an assessing manner that made Gideon wish he'd stayed outside. He'd met her grandfather only once and years ago. Would the old man remember him? Hopefully not.

Rebecca held out her hands. Her grandfather grasped them both and planted a kiss on each of her cheeks. He looked straight at Gideon. "And who is this?"

"This is Booker. He purchased my quilt at the auction yesterday."

"And paid a fine price for it, too, I hear."

"It was a fair price for a good cause." Gideon answered in his hoarse whisper.

The old man's bushy eyebrows shot upward. "You are ill?"

"I've lost my voice, that's all."

Nodding wisely, Reuben said, "I will keep a lookout for it."

Gideon cracked a smile. Rebecca giggled and said, "Booker, this is my grandfather, Reuben Beachy."

"God will bless your generosity, Booker. I pray with my whole heart that my granddaughter's vision may be restored."

"As do I," Gideon replied, gazing intently at the woman beside him.

She said, "*Aenti* Vera has sent me to tell you she needs a new set of driving lines for Boppli."

"Did your mare break another pair?"

"*Ja,* she can be headstrong at times," Rebecca admitted.

"Like her owners. Does Vera want leather or nylon reins this time?" Reuben placed her hand on his arm and led her toward the front of the store. Gideon tagged after them.

"*Aenti* says the nylon lines are lighter and easier for her to hold."

While Rebecca and Reuben chatted, Gideon walked among the harnesses displayed on curved wooden racks that simulated a horse's back. The quality of the workmanship was easy to see. As he stood admiring a leather horse collar, the front door opened and a man about Gideon's age walked in. He was dressed plain with a dark hat and dark clothing, but he was clean-shaven. Only married men wore beards. Gideon scratched the stubble on his cheeks.

"*Guder mariye,* Reuben," the stranger called out.

Gideon took a closer look at the man. His greeting in Pennsylvanian Dutch was right, but his accent was all wrong.

Reuben said, "Hello, Jonathan. What can I do for you today?"

"I got a new horse in yesterday and I need a collar and harness for him. He's a little fellow and none of mine will fit him. I have him outside. Is it all right if I try a couple on him?"

"Sure. A poor-fitting collar has damaged many a good horse. Make sure it isn't too big on him. Four fingers should fit snugly between his neck and the collar."

"I know. *Danki.* Hello, Rebecca." The stranger smiled warmly at her.

"Jonathan, how are you?"

"Cold. And you?"

"The same."

Gideon could tell by the tone of her voice that she was friends with this man. Close friends? How close?

He turned his back to the group. He was an intruder in their circle. An outsider. He had no reason to be jealous of Rebecca's friendship with this man, but annoyance pricked at him anyway.

When Reuben and Jonathan took their collars

outside, Gideon moved to stand by Rebecca. "Your friend looks Amish but he doesn't sound Amish."

"He was *Englisch,* but he has chosen to live among us and become one of us."

"That is a rare thing."

"*Ja,* it is. He has lived here for a year now and his Pennsylvania Dutch is pretty good. I think he will ask to be baptized soon."

"And then what?"

She leaned toward Gideon and whispered, "Hopefully, there will be a wedding in the fall."

"Yours?"

She straightened abruptly. "*Nee.* Jonathan is not courting me. He has his eye on my friend, Karen Imhoff."

Gideon was hard put to explain the rush of relief that filled him. "And does she have her eye on Jonathan?"

"Most definitely. Are you ready to go?"

"Where to next?"

"I am done with my errands, so it is back to the inn."

He didn't want their morning to end. "Do we really have to go back?"

He watched the uncertainty flit across her face. An instant later, her uncertainty vanished. "There is no rush. Do you have any shopping you would like to do?"

"I'll think of something."

Suddenly, a loud scraping noise reverberated through the building. Rebecca took a step closer to him and grasped his jacket sleeve. “What was that?”

“My guess? Snow and ice sliding off the roof.” He covered her hand with his.

She relaxed and pulled her hand away slowly. “Of course, how silly of me to be frightened.”

“Don’t apologize.”

Clearly flustered, she said, “I really should get back. My aunt will be waiting for me. We…we have plans for today.”

It took all his willpower to step away from her. “I understand.”

They crossed through the store to the back door, but when she tried to open it the door barely moved. “There’s something blocking it.”

He put his shoulder against it and pushed. It budged a few inches, enough for him to see it was snow blocking the door. The pile was at least four feet deep. “Looks like this is where the snow from the roof landed.”

“We can go out the other way.”

They returned to the front of the store. Jonathan had gone. Reuben was placing a number of bills in his cash register.

Rebecca said, “*Daadi,* the back door is blocked.”

“I heard the avalanche. I will take care of it.” Reuben sighed and moved to pick up a snow shovel by the front door.

Gideon stepped forward and took hold of the tool. "Let me do that for you."

Reuben frowned at him. "I can shovel a little snow."

"I can, too." Gideon grinned. The man must be close to eighty years old.

Reuben relinquished his hold. "*Danki,* Booker."

Gideon turned to Rebecca. "You should go back to the inn. I can find my way. I was only teasing you about being lost."

Her lips curved slightly. "I know. I don't mind waiting."

After Gideon left the building, Rebecca's grandfather spoke to her in Pennsylvania Dutch. "How well do you know this *Englisch* fellow?"

"We only met at the auction, but he has been most kind."

"Do I need to put a word of caution in your ear?" Reuben asked in a firm tone he rarely used with her.

Her pleasure dimmed. "No, *Daadi,* I know what is proper."

"I'm happy to hear that. Do not be fooled by his interest."

"I don't know what you mean." She did, but she didn't want to hear it put into words.

"You are a lovely woman. He is an outsider, stuck in our little town until the roads are clear. Do not be flattered by his attention. It will vanish when the roads are open."

Was she so pathetic? Tears pricked at the back of her eyes. "Is it wrong to show him kindness after all he has done for me? We took a walk through town. Nothing else."

Pressing her lips together, she waited for her grandfather to respond. How could it be wrong to enjoy a stroll with Booker? She knew nothing could come of the relationship. He made her feel special. He made her smile. Didn't she deserve a few hours of enjoyment?

"You are a grown woman with a *goot* head on your shoulders. I don't wish to see you hurt."

"When Jonathan came among us you were not suspicious of his motives."

"Jonathan was a man with no memory. He didn't know his own name. It was clear God brought him to us so that he might be healed in body and soul."

"Perhaps God has such a reason for bringing Booker here."

"That may be true, but Booker looks more like a man with something to hide than a man looking to find God's will."

"Why do you say that?"

"There is something about the way he doesn't look a man in the eye."

"Perhaps he's shy. Maybe he feels uncomfortable

because we look at him with suspicion." She felt compelled to defend Booker.

"Perhaps you are right and I am wrong to judge him harshly. 'It is better to suffer wrong than to do it.'"

"'And happier to be sometimes cheated than to never trust.'" She finished the proverb for him.

"All I'm trying to say is be careful, child."

"I will be, Grandfather. Don't worry."

Harness bells chimed as the front door opened. When the new arrival called a greeting in Pennsylvania Dutch Rebecca knew it wasn't Booker returning.

The customer was shopping for a new halter. Rebecca waited by the counter as her grandfather went to help him.

She had always heeded her grandfather's counsel, so why was she unwilling to do so now? He thought it unwise of her to spend time with Booker. One day spent in the company of a man who found her companionship pleasant. Where was the harm in that?

She knew. She didn't want to admit it, but she knew. The harm was in wanting more than one day with such a man.

She had been foolish. It was time to go back to the life she was meant to lead. Skating on thin ice would only lead to a cold bath.

"Tell Booker that I changed my mind. I've decided to return to the inn after all."

"That is a wise decision, child. Give Vera my love and tell her you are both invited to supper come Sunday."

"I'm afraid we have other plans."

"Oh?"

"Daniel Hershburger has already invited us to eat with him and his sister."

"Has he, now? Well, well. He is a fine man, a devout man. I'm glad to hear this. You and Vera must come by some evening when you are free. Why don't you invite Daniel, too? I haven't had a good game of checkers in a long while. What do you think of that idea?"

She forced herself to smile. "I think it sounds fine, *Daadi.*"

Chapter Six

When Gideon finished his labor, he opened the back door of the harness shop and carried the snow shovel through the building. Rebecca's grandfather sat behind the counter on a tall stool tooling a length of harness. He looked up when he heard Gideon and nodded. "*Danki,* your help is appreciated."

"I'm happy to do it." Gideon's voice was barely audible and the sensation of swallowing razor blades was back. He looked around but didn't see Rebecca.

"My granddaughter decided to go back to the inn," Reuben said before Gideon could ask.

Gideon tried to hide his disappointment. Reuben returned to his work without another word. Recognizing a dismissal when he saw it, Gideon walked out the front door. Had he made trouble for Rebecca? He knew a few Amish elders who would see her casual friendship with him as brazen behavior.

Standing on the sidewalk, he pushed his hands

deeper into his coat pockets. The day seemed colder without Rebecca's company. He had worked up a sweat shoveling. Now a chill was setting in.

Traffic had picked up on the streets. Chances were good that the interstate would be open soon, if it wasn't already. The narrow rural highway between Hope Springs and the interstate might be another story, but Gideon found he wasn't eager to leave the quiet village.

Okay, he wasn't eager to leave Rebecca. The connection was still there between them. He felt it. The question was—what should he do about it?

He shook his head at his foolishness. What was the point of resurrecting his emotions from their old relationship when Rebecca had no idea who he was? He wasn't being fair to her or to himself. Suddenly he realized how tired he was. His illness had seriously sapped his energy. His good deed of shoveling aside four feet of packed snow had burned through what little he had left.

Or maybe it was his guilty conscience making him tired. Pretending to be someone he wasn't was harder than he thought. With heavy steps, he started walking toward the inn.

By the time he reached the building he was ready to crawl under the covers and hide. He wasn't in any shape to attempt the six-hour drive home. When he entered the lobby, he was relieved to see his cousin wasn't on duty. The elderly man behind the desk was the same fellow that checked Gideon in. He wasn't Amish.

"Did you enjoy your stay with us, Mr. Troyer?"

Gideon glanced around to see who might have overheard his name. There was no one about. He managed a smile and said, "Call me Booker. It's a very comfortable place. I know I'm due to check out today, but is there any way I can stay another night?"

"Certainly. I can keep you in the same room for two more days if you like."

"One more will be fine." Relieved, Gideon climbed the stairs and walked slowly down the hall. At the door to Rebecca's room he paused. He considered knocking to see if she had made it back okay but decided against it. It would be better all around if he let their budding relationship die a natural death. As far as she knew they were two strangers staying at the same inn. They had enjoyed a walk together and nothing more. He should let it go at that.

He needed to let go of her.

Unlocking his own door, he entered the cozy room where an old-fashioned four-poster bed with a blue-and-white quilted coverlet was calling his name. He tossed his coat over a chair, kicked off his shoes and lay down fully dressed on the bed. After a minute, he rolled to his side and dragged the corner of the bedspread across his shoulders.

The next time he opened his eyes the room was completely dark. Squinting at the clock on the bedside table, he saw it was nearly eleven-thirty at night and he was starving. Had he really slept for twelve hours?

It was too late to call Roseanne or Craig now. He'd have to try to catch them early in the morning to let them know he wouldn't be back until the day after tomorrow. Although the company had three flights booked for the next two days, Craig would just have to pick up the slack.

Gideon sat up and rubbed his gritty eyes. His chin itched. He ran a hand over his bristly cheeks and scratched his face. He needed a shave. A few more days and he could pass for an Amish newlywed. He'd be glad when his halfhearted disguise wasn't needed anymore.

Rising, he moved to the window and looked out. At least it wasn't snowing. From his vantage point he could see the outline of the shops across the street highlighted by a red glow behind them. It took his sleep-stupid brain a full ten seconds to process what he was seeing.

There was a building on fire.

Dashing back to the bed, he grabbed the phone on the nightstand and dialed 911, praying this sleepy little town had an emergency dispatch. To his relief, a woman's voice said, "911 operator. What is your emergency?"

He tried to speak, but his voice failed him. Apparently, getting chilled had set back his recovery.

"What is your emergency?" the woman asked, louder this time.

He tried harder, straining his vocal cords. "I can see a building on fire from my window."

"I'm sorry, I can't understand you. Would you repeat that, please?"

He dropped the receiver beside the phone and headed out the door. He had to find someone with a voice. In the dark hallway, he saw a sliver of light coming from beneath Rebecca's door. He pounded on the wooden panel.

When there was no response, he knocked again. This time, he heard her uncertain voice. "Who is it?"

"It's Booker." Great, he couldn't identify himself beyond a harsh whisper he doubted she could hear through the thick door. He knocked again.

The door opened a crack. "Booker? Is that you?"

He drew his hand across his throat hoping she would understand he couldn't talk and then realized she couldn't see him, either. He swallowed hard and struggled to speak. "Rebecca, I need your help."

The door opened wide. She stood with a soft blue robe pulled over her floor-length white nightgown. Her hair was in a long braid hanging over her shoulder. He had been right. It was past her waist now. She stared sightlessly past him.

He leaned forward, close to her ear and whispered, "I see a building on fire from my window."

From inside the room, he heard her aunt call out. "Rebecca, what's going on? It's nearly midnight."

"Booker says he sees a building on fire."

"Where?"

They were wasting valuable time. Gideon took Rebecca's hand and pulled her across the hall to his room. Picking up the phone, he placed it to her ear and said, "Tell them."

Clearly, the 911 operator was still on the line. Rebecca said, "Hello, this is Rebecca Beachy. I want to report a fire."

Gideon placed his ear on the outside of the receiver to hear the woman's response.

"Can you give me your address?"

"I'm staying at the Wadler Inn in Hope Springs."

"Is the fire at the inn?"

Gideon said no and Rebecca repeated the information.

"Can you give me the location of the fire?"

By this time Rebecca's aunt had followed them into the room. Gideon led her to his window. Now that the women would be able to stay on the line with the dispatcher, he could go get more help. He pulled on his shoes and grabbed his coat.

Rebecca said, "They're putting a call into the Hope Springs volunteer fire department. They will be on their way soon, but they need an address."

Gideon pointed to himself then to the fire and retrieved his cell phone. Vera nodded in understanding. She said, "Rebecca, tell them Mr. Booker is heading toward the fire now. He'll have someone call them on his cell phone. I'll rouse the house."

Gideon grabbed his coat and sprinted out the door. At the foot of the stairs, he looked back once and saw Vera coming down, too. She would raise the alarm and get help from the staff at the inn.

Outside, he raced across the street and followed the same path he and Rebecca had walked that morning. As he ran down the sidewalk a sick feeling settled in the pit of his stomach. He wasn't sure until he passed the fabric shop and reached the alley they had taken to her grandfather's shop. Through the narrow walkway he saw the flames licking up the back wall of the harness shop. The snow-covered ground reflected the dancing orange glow. The stench of smoke fouled the night air.

Gideon hurried down the alley. Already the heat had broken out several windows at the rear of the building. No one was about yet. The windows of the homes on either side of the building were dark. It wasn't going to take much for the fire to spread across the narrow spaces between the wooden structures. He had to wake people.

Looking around he spotted a metal trash can at the side of the alley. He picked up the lid and started banging it against the can for all he was worth. It seemed like an eternity before the back door of one house finally opened and an irate voice shouted, "Knock off that racket!"

From above, he heard a window open. This time a woman screeched, "Fire!"

Now that he was sure the alarm would be spread, Gideon dropped his noisemaker and raced around to the front of the building. The shop was adjacent to Reuben's home. He had to make sure the elderly couple was safe.

Reuben's home was dark, but Gideon saw someone standing in the street in front of it. It wasn't Reuben. The bystander was a boy of about sixteen. He already had his cell phone to his ear. Trusting that the boy was calling 911, Gideon sprinted up the steps of Reuben's house and began pounding on the door. The flames were clearly visible over the roof of the shop now.

He was ready to break down the door when Reuben finally appeared. He held a battery-powered lantern in his hand. Raising it high, he squinted at Gideon. "What is the meaning of this?"

The boy from the street ran up. "Mr. Beachy, your shop is on fire."

Reuben's eyes widened. "*Gott,* have mercy."

He turned back into the house and Gideon heard him shouting for his wife. In the distance, he heard the faint wail of sirens. Help was on its way at last.

A moment later, Reuben came out of his house pulling his coat over his nightclothes. He hurried past Gideon to the front door of his shop, opened it and disappeared inside.

"Is the old man crazy?" the boy standing beside Gideon asked in astonishment.

The Amish didn't believe in insurance. Reuben had to save as much of his merchandise as he could. Knowing that it was the stupidest thing he had ever done, Gideon followed Rebecca's grandfather into the harness shop.

Rebecca learned it was her grandfather's shop nearly thirty minutes after Booker left her. Having returned to their room and dressed, she and Vera were in the lobby of the inn when word reached them by way of Naomi Wadler.

Now, an hour later, the three women were in the kitchen preparing thermoses of coffee and sandwiches that would be taken to the volunteers working to contain the blaze.

The back door of the kitchen banged open. Naomi asked, "What news is there, Kyle?"

A young boy's voice answered, "The roof just fell in. You should've seen the sparks fly."

Rebecca didn't share young Kyle's sense of excitement. She wished the news had been better. "Are you sure my *daadi* is all right?"

"He's fine, but Adrian says the shop can't be saved. They're still trying to keep it from spreading to Reuben's house and some others."

Adrian Lapp, Kyle's stepfather, was one of the volunteer firefighters. Word had spread slowly since most Amish families lived without telephones, but within an hour men from miles around were pouring in to help. The street in front of the inn was lined with buggies and hastily saddled horses.

Vera said, "It's a blessing there is so much snow on the roofs. It may help stop the fire from spreading."

"Has anyone been hurt?" Naomi asked.

Kyle said, "I seen Dr. White and his nurse taking care of somebody. Don't know who it was."

Rebecca screwed the lid on the thermos she had just filled and handed it to Kyle. "Have you seen an *Englisch* fellow named Booker?"

"Maybe. There's lots of *Englisch* there, too. I got to go." The slamming of the back door told Rebecca he was gone.

"I'm sure Booker is fine." Vera patted Rebecca's hand.

A few moments later, the back door opened again. "Naomi, have you any more cups?" This time it was Faith Lapp, Kyle's mother. Although she and her adopted son were new to the area, they had quickly become well-loved members of the Hope Springs community. Perhaps she had more information.

Naomi said, "*Ja,* I have stacks of foam cups in the pantry. I'll get them."

Rebecca asked, "Faith, could you check on a

man named Booker for us? He has been staying at the inn. He's the one who spotted the fire and we haven't heard from him since."

"Of course. I'll send Kyle with news when I have it. Is he the fellow that bought your quilt?"

"Ja." Rebecca prayed he was safe. Why hadn't he come back?

She heard Naomi return. "Faith, I have extra blankets and quilts if you need them. I have empty rooms, too, if someone needs a place to stay."

"*Danki,* at least four families have had to evacuate their homes. I will see if they want to bring the children here. The men are busy trying to save what furnishing they can."

"Has anyone been hurt?" Vera asked. Rebecca held her breath waiting for an answer.

"A few minor burns. Your father breathed in too much smoke, but the doctor says he will be fine. Someone pulled him out of the building in the nick of time."

"Praise the Lord." Vera's voice broke and she started to cry. Rebecca slipped her arms around Vera's shoulders to offer what comfort she could.

Faith's voice softened. "His wife was busy scolding him for his foolishness when I left."

Vera sniffed once and chuckled. "My stepmother is a wise woman. Better than Papa deserves. God is *goot.*"

"*Ja.* He has been merciful tonight," Faith added.

The sound of the back door closing told Rebecca Faith was gone.

"I should gather those blankets together in case they are needed," Naomi announced.

"Let me get them," Rebecca offered. She needed to keep busy.

"The linen room is the last door on the left at the end of the hall upstairs. Any of them will do."

"I'll find them." Rebecca made her way upstairs and located the room without difficulty. The linens were stored on open shelves, making it easy for her to find blankets by feel. Gathering a large armload, she started back down the hall. Suddenly, she caught the sharp smell of smoke and soot.

She stopped in her tracks. A second later, she heard muffled footsteps. "Is someone there?"

"Just me."

His harsh whisper sent joy leaping through her chest. "Booker, are you all right?"

"I'm fine."

"You smell terrible."

"Like charred barbecue?" His laugh turned into a cough.

"Are you truly okay?" She tried to tell herself she was worried about everyone who was battling the fire, but the truth was she cared about Booker more than she should.

"I'm fine. Don't worry about me."

She was thankful for the load of blankets in her

arms. They kept her from reaching out and "seeing" for herself with her hands that he was unharmed. Gripping the stack tighter, she asked, "Is the blaze out?"

"Not out but under control. A second fire company arrived from Sugarcreek. They sent a lot of us home."

"My grandfather?"

"He's one tough old bird. His house was damaged, but it won't take much to repair. He and his wife are downstairs. I think they plan to stay here tonight."

"I heard his shop is completely gone."

"Ja."

She smiled. "*Ja?* You've been hanging around us Amish too long."

"Maybe so."

An awkward silence stretched between them. She shifted the load in her arms. "Are you leaving tomorrow?"

"That's the plan."

"Back to soaring with the birds?"

"Something like that."

She nodded. He had to leave sooner or later. She had to stay. Drawing a deep breath, she said, "I need to get these downstairs. Come down when you've cleaned up and I'll fix you a sandwich and some tea."

"I'm not hungry. I just want to turn in."

"Of course. We owe you a debt of gratitude, Booker. Had you not seen the fire when you did, lives may have been lost."

"It was nothing."

"God brought you here for a reason. I think this was it."

She heard him sigh. Quietly, he whispered, "Good night, Rebecca."

"*Guten nacht*, Booker. Sleep well."

She heard the door to his room open and close. She stood in the hall for another minute to compose herself, then she went downstairs to join her family.

"I owe you much, Booker." Reuben Beachy stroked his beard and then pushed the brim of his dark hat up with one finger.

"Next time run out of a burning building instead of into it." Gideon's voice was making a comeback. He sounded almost like himself this afternoon. He would have to be careful if he spoke to Rebecca again.

He could see her working along the women who were helping sort and clean the merchandise he and Reuben had carried out before the roof fell in. The memory of the smoke burning his lungs and eyes as he dragged out tools and materials was one he'd rather forget. He glanced down at the bandage on his left arm. He would always have a scar to remind him of his visit to Hope Springs.

All morning long teams of horses and wagons had hauled away loads of charred debris. By noon the old foundation stones of the building had been washed down and made ready to bear a new structure. After that, wagonloads of lumber and building materials began to arrive along with several truckloads donated by the local lumberyard. The sounds of hammers and saws echoed off the surrounding buildings. Everyone, Amish and English townspeople alike, were pitching in to help one of their own recover from a disaster.

Well over fifty men continued working in the cold afternoon air while the women supplied them with hot drinks and food of every sort from roast pork sandwiches to chocolate chip cookies and whoopie pies. The army of denim-clad Amish farmers and carpenters in black hats and tool belts swarmed over the site like bees over a honeycomb. By four o'clock the skeleton of a new building was rising against the blue sky.

As Gideon stood beside Reuben, two dozen of Reuben's Amish neighbors prepared to lift a twenty-five-foot beam into the building they were raising where only ashes lay the night before.

When the beam settled safely into place, Reuben turned to Gideon. He cleared his throat. "I misjudged you, English. I warned my granddaughter against you. I would do so again, but I would not mistrust your motives in being kind to her. I owe you my life."

Reuben's unconscious body was the last thing Gideon had carried out of the burning shop. It had been a close call. "You are concerned about Rebecca. I understand and respect that. I'm just sorry you lost your business."

"*So ist das Leben.* Such is life!" Reuben declared. "I am a man blessed."

"How can you say that when all you worked for is gone?"

"Look about you. Why should I feel sorrow? My children and grandchildren, my friends and my neighbors are here to help. I could not survive without them or without my faith in God. The things I lost are merely…things. I do not worry about tomorrow—too much. That is in God's hands."

Someone called Reuben away. Gideon knew that within a week Reuben would be open for business again. It might take him a while to replace his large inventory and machinery, but he wasn't the kind of man to quit because things were hard.

Gideon took his time getting back to the inn. When he stepped inside, he saw Adam carrying a pair of suitcases. Approaching his cousin, Gideon said, "Adam, I need you to do something for me."

"I go out of town for two days and look what happens. I understand we have you to thank for spotting the fire before it had a chance to spread. God was with you. How is Reuben?"

"He's tough. He'll get through this."

"What can I do for you?"

"I want to give Rebecca's quilt to you. I want you to sell it again and give the money to Reuben to help him rebuild."

"That is a generous thing, Gideon."

"It's the least I can do."

"My wife and I are leaving this evening to visit your folks for a few days and share our good news."

"What news?"

"We are expecting our first child."

"Wow. Congratulations. That's wonderful."

"I would be happy to take a letter to your mother, if you'd like to write one."

Gideon met Adam's gaze. Maybe it was time he tried making amends. A letter to his family would be a good place to start. "I would appreciate that."

Adam's eyes brightened. "You mean it? You will write?"

"I'm not sure what I will say."

"Say what is in your heart, cousin."

"I'll try."

Thirty minutes later, Gideon met Adam in the lobby again. He laid an envelope on the front desk and shoved his hands in his pockets. "It's a long overdue apology. I expect my mother will cry."

"This is a good thing, Gideon."

"If I went for a visit, do you think I could meet my nephews and nieces?"

"I will ask. Those that have not been baptized are free to speak with you."

"Only if their parents let them."

"As I said, I will ask. And I will tell them the good you have done here."

The letter wasn't much, but it was a start. Gideon tried not to get his hopes up, but the thought of seeing his family again suddenly made him as homesick as he'd been the first week after he left.

Rebecca was right. He'd been hanging around the Amish too long. Their focus on God, family and community had him realizing how shallow his life was. He heard the front door of the inn open. He looked over as Rebecca walked in. The sight of her lifted his spirits.

She carried a large woven hamper with one arm. Gideon rushed toward her. "Let me give you a hand with that."

"*Danki,* Booker." She smiled at him as if she could see him.

His heart turned over in his chest. If he told her the truth, confessed his sins and begged her forgiveness, could he have the life he once turned his back on? Could he find happiness living among the Amish? Was this what God wanted for him?

To return to the Amish would mean giving up flying. How could he do that? If Rebecca knew the truth could he convince her to leave this life behind? What did she have? A close family, yes, but not children, not a husband. She deserved more.

Tell her. Tell her who you are.

Before he could open his mouth, his cell phone rang. Annoyed at the interruption, he pulled it out intending to silence it. When he saw the number was Roseanne's home phone, he frowned. He snapped open the phone. "What's going on, Roseanne?"

"Gideon, how soon can you get back here?"

"I was thinking about staying a few more days."

"No. You have to come back now."

A pit of fear formed in his midsection. "You're scaring me, Roseanne. What's wrong?"

"It's Craig. His plane is missing. He left here five hours ago and never reached his destination. He hasn't been heard from since he took off."

Chapter Seven

Rebecca listened to Booker rattling off instructions to the person on the phone. She wasn't sure what was wrong but she heard the distress in his voice. When he ended the call, she asked, "What has happened?"

"My partner has been making flights that I was supposed to make so I could stay here. Now the plane is missing. If anything has happened to him..." His voice trailed off.

"I pray he is safe, but he is in God's hands. You must not despair."

"I've forgotten what that is like."

"I don't understand."

"Accepting that everything is God's will. I've forgotten what that's like. I have to get back to Rochester."

"The Lord is our strength and our salvation, Booker. Lean on Him, for He loves all His children. Though we may not understand His plan for us, never doubt that He has one."

"I want to thank you, Rebecca."

"For what?"

"Let's just say for helping me realize some important truths. I wanted to say more, but to explain would take more time than I have now. I guess it wasn't meant to be. I've got to get going."

His voice was stronger today and more familiar. How was it that he seemed to grow more important to her with each passing minute? She listened to his footsteps bounding up the stairs. He would be gone as soon as he could pack and she would never spend time with him again.

"Is something wrong?" Adam asked. She hadn't heard him approach.

"Booker has to leave. His friend is in trouble."

"Is there anything we can do?"

"No, he is going home."

A car horn honked outside. Adam called out, "Emma, our driver is here."

"Coming." The rapid tapping of sturdy heels on the plank floor signaled Emma's approach. Breathlessly, she asked, "Did you tell Rebecca?"

"Tell me what?"

"The fellow who bought your quilt had donated it to help raise money for your grandfather. What a nice man he is. He reminds me of you, Adam."

"Come," Adam cut her short. "We mustn't keep the car waiting."

"All right. Goodbye, Rebecca. It was wonderful having you and your aunt here. I only wish we could have spent more time together."

"Goodbye. Have a safe trip," Rebecca called after them as they left.

Quiet filled the lobby. Rebecca listened for the sound of Booker coming down, but heard only the quiet ticking of the grandfather clock.

Would Booker think of her sometimes when he was gone from this place? He would have nothing to remember her by. He had given her quilt away.

She would have liked to think of him wrapped up in the comfort of her creation. She was sorry he decided to part with it, but she was thankful for his kindness toward her grandfather.

The clock began to strike the hour.

What was she thinking? Booker might not have the quilt from the auction, but he could still have one of hers. She'd finished her Christmas Star quilt late last night, placing her signature in Braille with French knots in the last square as she did with all her quilts. She knew God would direct her gift where it was needed the most.

She crossed the lobby quickly and found the stairs with her cane. Tucking her stick under her arm, she hurried up the steps.

The quilt was where she had left it, folded neatly

in a box beside her bed. She lifted the lid of the box and ran her hand across the folded fabric.

She tried to imagine how it must look. Her aunt told her it was made up of green, red and gold colors that formed a many-pointed star on a cream background. She tried to imagine it but her memory of colors was fading. Was the green the color of spring grass or the color of the summer woods?

It didn't matter. All that mattered was that her work brought joy or comfort to someone. To Booker. Gathering it in her arms, she started toward the door but paused with her hand on the cool metal knob.

Would he accept it? It was a valuable item in his eyes. He'd paid dearly for her previous work.

Perhaps he would think she was too forward in giving him such a gift. It was forward and unlike her.

She heard the sound of a door opening across the hall. It was now or never. Either she could let Booker walk away or she could open the door. The choice was hers. She took a deep breath and turned the handle. "Booker, is that you?"

She stood waiting for an answer. She knew he was in the hall with her. She could smell his cologne, she could hear his breathing. Why didn't he speak?

Gathering her courage, she took a step closer. "I have something for you."

"Why are you doing this?" His raspy voice held a note of pain.

"Doing what?" Hurting him was the last thing she wanted to do.

"Why are you making it so hard for me to leave?"

"I didn't realize I was."

"If only this had been another place, another time."

He stepped closer. She knew if she stretched out her hand she could touch him. She locked her fingers together beneath the quilt she held. "I don't know what you mean."

"Yes, you do. You are woman enough to know exactly what I mean. You feel it, too, this bond we have."

She did feel it, but she could never admit it. She smiled sadly. "Another time and another place would not have mattered, Booker. You come from a world I could not inhabit. I live where everyone's feet are planted firmly on the earth."

"I would stay, but my friend needs me."

"Go to him. I belong here."

"There's nothing for you here. No husband, no children, no ties that can't be broken. You could step into the world I come from. You could know freedom. I could find you the best medical care. You wouldn't have to work your fingers to the bone stitching quilts year after year."

Rebecca shook her head and clutched her quilt

tightly. "There are ties you cannot see, Booker. My soul is tied to God and to my people through my faith. I could no more break those cords than I could fly."

"I could take you flying. You could see the tops of the clouds and…" His voice trailed away, as if he'd forgotten her blindness for a moment and suddenly realized how foolish his words sounded.

She took pity on him. "I have no wish to fly, Booker. That is for the birds of the air."

He sighed deeply. "I hope you're not offended by my offer."

She bowed her head hoping he would not notice the heat rushing to her cheeks. "*Nee,* I shall cherish it as the wish of one friend to aid another."

To her surprise, he slipped his fingers under her chin and raised her face. Her heart pounded so hard she thought he must hear it. If only she could see his face.

He said, "I could have been more than a friend to you…in another time and in another place."

Swallowing hard, she struggled to keep her voice steady. "I know you gave away the quilt you bought."

He took his hand away from her face. She missed the warmth and gentleness of his touch. He said, "I wish now that I hadn't. You're a very remarkable woman, Rebecca."

She struggled to maintain her composure. "It is

not my goal to be remarkable. It is my goal to be a humble servant of God."

"And that is the goal of all Amish. Am I right?"

"Ja." She extended the quilt toward him. "This is my gift to you. Please take it and remember me with kindness whenever you see it."

To her relief, he took the quilt from her. She stepped back a pace. "May God go with you, Booker, whether your feet be on the ground or skipping across the clouds above."

She turned away, found the doorknob of her room with trembling hands and entered with tears stinging her eyes. She leaned against the door and wondered if God would forgive her for wanting to go with him.

Hours later, Gideon learned Craig and the plane had been found following a crash landing. His friend was alive, but their plane wasn't in one piece. After hearing the details from Roseanne, Gideon knew exactly how lucky his friend had been.

Gideon pushed open the door of the hospital room and stepped inside. The lights had been turned down low and the shades were drawn. Craig lay with his eyes closed on the crisp white sheets. A thick bandage covered the right side of his head.

Gideon might have thought he was sleeping except that his hands were clenching into tight fists.

Stepping closer, Gideon said, "I thought the idea was to keep our planes in one piece."

Craig opened his eyes. "Look what the cat dragged in."

"How you doing?"

Craig grimaced. "I've been better."

"You can have pain medication. You don't have to tough it out."

"They just gave me something. I don't like whatever it is. It makes me go to sleep and then I get these awful nightmares. How bad is the plane?"

Gideon saw no reason to sugarcoat it. "A total loss. How bad are you?"

"I'm not as pretty as I was before. I think they put twenty stitches in my forehead. My ribs are bruised. My ankle is sprained, not broken. That's the good news. They want to keep me overnight for observation. I'm sorry. This is gonna set us back."

"Don't worry about it. We have one plane left and our insurance will go a long way toward getting us a replacement for the one you ditched in the lake."

"I put her down on the shore. It if hadn't been for the boulders that jumped into my path, I would have made a fine landing."

"You were lucky to get out in one piece. Just mend and get back in the air. Unless this has put you off flying."

"Are you kidding? You think one little crash is

gonna ground me for good? Not hardly. I'll be back up there before you know it."

"It wasn't a little crash, Craig."

His gaze grew pensive. "Yeah, I know. I saw the ground coming up and...I wasn't ready."

"You weren't ready for what?"

"I wasn't ready to die. In that second, man, I knew my time was up, and I hadn't done the one thing I needed to do. I didn't want to die without telling a certain person how much she means to me, how much I love her."

"I can pass that sentiment on to Roseanne if you like."

Craig laughed then grimaced as he clutched his sides. "Don't do that. Don't make me laugh. It hurts."

"Then I will tell you that Melody is outside with Roseanne. She got here a couple minutes after I did."

"She's here?" Craig's pain-filled expression lightened for an instant then darkened again.

Gideon studied Craig's face. Softly, he asked, "What happened? I thought you and Melody were doing great."

"I thought we were, too. She has a kid, Gideon."

"And you just found this out?"

"Yeah. Apparently, my reaction to the news wasn't all she hoped it would be. It got a little ugly.

I said some things, she said some things. The whole argument was totally stupid."

"I'm sorry, Craig."

"Me, too. Don't get me wrong. I've thought about having kids, but I thought…someday, not right now. Then yesterday, all my somedays came real close to being never. I got a second chance. Do you know how rare that is, Gideon? God gave me a second chance to try and make things right."

Gideon did understand. God had given him a second chance to know Rebecca. She wasn't the girl he left behind. She had become a strong woman, steadfast in her faith in spite of her trials. He admired her with a newfound respect and longed to see her again, but Craig's chances of a happy reunion were much better.

Gideon said, "I know how rare second chances are. I also know that Melody would like to see you. Shall I have her come in?"

"What if I mess this up? What if she can't forgive me? What if she thinks I'll make a lousy father? Will I?"

His friend's dilemma wasn't something Gideon could answer. Having a family and kids had fallen off his radar years ago. "I think if you love each other you'll find a way to make it work."

Craig fixed his gaze on the door. "Booker, if it had been you going down in the plane, would you have had regrets?"

Rebecca's face came back to haunt Gideon. "I would have my share."

"Was the Amish woman on television one of them?"

"It's complicated, Craig." Complicated and hopeless.

Craig put his head back and closed his eyes. "Want some advice from a guy who saw his life flash before his eyes? Don't wait until your plane is going down to think about making things right."

"I'll let Melody come in now." Gideon opened the door and stepped outside. Melody stood in the hallway with Roseanne. The fear and worry etched on her young face told Gideon everything he needed to know about her feelings for Craig.

He said, "He'd like to see you now. His pain medication is making him a little groggy. In case he falls asleep before he has a chance to tell you he was a jerk, I'm telling you now he knows he was."

A smile trembled briefly on her lips. "I can put up with a man who's a jerk once in a while as long as he's alive."

After she went in and closed the door, Gideon slipped his hands in the front pockets of his jeans and faced Roseanne. "It should've been me. I should've made that flight."

Roseanne shook her head. "Everything happens for a reason, Gideon. There was a reason Craig was in the plane. There was a reason you were stranded in a little town in Ohio. We just don't always get to know what those reasons are."

"With only one plane we aren't going to have much business."

"Maybe now I can get caught up on my paperwork. Our insurance will take care of another plane. Isn't that why we pay those outlandish premiums?"

"Yes, but that will take time."

A couple came down the hall toward them and Gideon realized they were Craig's parents. There was a strong family resemblance between father and son. Funny, he had known Craig for five years and had never met his family. Such a thing would have been inconceivable in the close-knit Amish community where Gideon grew up.

Everyone knew everyone. Members took turns hosting church services in each other's homes. One family's troubles belonged to all. He had only to think about Reuben's fire to know the truth of that. The waiting room would have been filled to overflowing with concerned and prayerful parents, siblings, aunts, uncles and cousins if an Amish man had been as seriously injured as Craig had been.

If it had been Gideon in that room, would his family have come had they known? Would they be there to pray for him and to urge him to come back to God and his faith?

Craig's father, a distinguished-looking man with wings of silver at his temples, stopped beside them. Craig's mother, a dainty woman barely five feet tall, clutched her husband's arm.

Gideon extended his hand to Craig's father. "Hello, sir. I'm Gideon Troyer, Craig's partner."

Craig's mother asked, "Where is he? How badly is he hurt? We couldn't get any information."

Gideon smiled to reassure her. "He's pretty banged up. He has a mild concussion, some bruised ribs and a sprained ankle, but he's going to be fine."

Craig's father looked relieved but his mother's worried expression didn't change. "Can I see him?"

"Sure, go on in."

As the couple stepped past them and entered the room, Roseanne asked, "Should I have warned them about Melody?"

"No, Craig's a big boy."

Don't wait until your plane is going down to make things right.

Craig's words repeated in Gideon's mind, then he thought, *I knew before I left Hope Springs what I wanted to do. I reckon now is the time to do it. Craig will do okay without me. He has a good head for business. Roseanne will help him every step of the way.*

"What's the matter, Gideon? You've been different since you came back from Ohio." Roseanne was studying him intently.

"I know."

"This wasn't your fault, if that's what's troubling you."

"No, it's not Craig. He's going to be fine."

A sudden rush of excitement mushroomed in Gideon's body. Was it possible? Could he go back and make a life for himself within the Amish community? Could he humble himself before the church and admit he'd made a bad decision? Would he be forgiven and welcomed by his family after so long?

He'd gone into the outside world determined to leave his Amish past behind. Until he'd gone to Hope Springs, he didn't realize what a hole leaving his faith made inside of him. Yes, he missed Rebecca, but he missed his family, too. He missed his father's stern teachings and his mother's warmhearted kindness. He loved them, and he'd cut himself off out of false pride.

He missed feeling at one with God and his community. Yes, he'd become a successful man, but at what cost to his soul? He could go back. He could make amends for everything he'd done. If he didn't go now, it might be too late.

It was a huge step. There would be no turning back if he took it. He had broken his vow once before. He wouldn't do it again, but was he considering this only because of Rebecca? What if she wasn't interested in sharing his life?

But what if she was?

He made up his mind and a weight lifted from his soul. He smiled at his secretary. "Roseanne, you've been a good friend as well as a good employee. When the insurance check comes in I want you to make sure Craig gets a good deal on a sound plane."

"Sure, but where will you be?"

"I'm going back to Ohio."

"For how long?"

"I'm going back for good."

Her eyes widened in disbelief. "To the Amish? Why?"

"Because I made a mistake a long time ago. I feel I've been given a chance to make that right. When Craig is up and around, I'll talk to him about buying out my half of the company. I know he can handle it. I've got to sell my car and get rid of the stuff at my apartment. You can have anything you like from the place."

"Gideon, you can't just leave us."

He leaned forward and kissed her cheek. "Keep the knucklehead in line."

"Thank you for coming in today, Rebecca." Dr. Harold White pulled his chair closer to her.

"I was surprised to get your message." Rebecca, perched on an exam table in the Hope Springs medical clinic, couldn't help wondering why she was here.

"I received a surprising call from my grandson yesterday evening."

Dr. Philip White was completing his internship in genetic studies at the University of Cleveland. It had been Philip who mentioned Rebecca's case to a visiting eye surgeon at the clinic. He had been instrumental in convincing the surgeon, Dr. Tuva Eriksson, to see Rebecca.

She said, "I hope Dr. Philip is well?"

"He's fine. The reason he called has to do with you. It seems Dr. Eriksson's clinic in New York has received a substantial donation of money toward your upcoming surgery. In fact, your procedure is now tentatively scheduled for the week before Christmas."

"My surgery has been approved?" Rebecca couldn't believe what she was hearing.

"Yes."

Joy followed by abject terror poured through her body. "It's all paid for?"

"The donation, along with the money that has been raised here, will cover the cost of your surgery and hospital stay. Dr. Eriksson has offered to waive her fee. You are all set."

"Who has done this? Who sent them so much money?"

"Someone who wished to remain anonymous."

"I don't know what to say." Her head was in a whirl.

"That's why you're here today. Are you ready to start the preparations and treatment we talked about?"

"Am I ready to begin chemotherapy?" Dr. White had already explained the powerful drugs were needed to decrease the inflammation the disease produced inside her eyes. Like a cancer, her cells had gone haywire making her blind.

"Dr. Eriksson feels unless we begin soon, we won't be able to reduce the inflammation in your eyes enough to have the surgery. A lot hinges on your response to these two drugs. I must tell you, I'm no expert on this type of thing."

"I understand. Dr. Eriksson explained there is no assurance of success. It is an experimental surgery and has only been tried a few times before."

The doctor took her hand. "There is less than a fifty percent chance that this will work, Rebecca. I don't know how to tell you not to get your hopes up."

She managed a lopsided grin. "Are you telling me that this surgery could leave me blind? Doctor, I'm already blind."

"I know you're trying to make light of the situation, but the truth is, this procedure could prevent any hope of a cure in the future. New research on uveitis could uncover a better procedure or better medication in the near future. Research is ongoing in the field."

"I pray a cure is discovered, for I am not the only person with this disease. When do we start?"

"Today. I'm going to read you this consent. You must sign it before we can start the medications. I want you to stop me if you have any questions. I'm going to have your aunt step in now, if that's all right? She should hear this, too."

With her aunt at her side, Rebecca listened as the doctor described the side effects she was likely to have on the chemotherapy. Although the dosages of the drugs were much smaller than when they were used to treat cancer, she might still be affected with nausea, vomiting, headaches, body aches and more. The list went on and on. He made it clear she might endure all the side effects and still not be able to have her surgery.

Was it worth it? She was accustomed to being in the dark. For a moment she was tempted to back out, to return to her aunt's home and live there quietly until the end of her days. Then she recalled Booker's voice as he talked about looking down from the clouds. She would never look down from the clouds, but she would give anything to look up and see them in the sky overhead once more.

After the doctor finished, Rebecca signed her name where he indicated and tried to still her racing heart. It was finally going to happen thanks to an anonymous donor. In her heart, she knew the money had come from Booker. She would be forever in his debt.

That afternoon and forty miles away, Gideon sat in the front seat of Roseanne's car as she turned onto a farm lane outside Berlin, Ohio. His hands grew cold as ice as his heart pounded like a runaway train. He was here. This was the exact place where his Amish life had ended. It seemed fitting that this was where his English life would end, as well.

He said, "Stop here."

Roseanne shot him a funny look. "Don't you want me to drive up to the house?"

"No. I want to walk."

"It's freezing outside."

"I'll be fine."

She stopped the car and put it in Park. "Are you sure about this, Gideon?"

He knew she wasn't asking about his hike up the lane. Laying a hand on her shoulder, he said, "I'll be fine, Roseanne. This is what I want."

She sniffed and wiped her eyes. "If you ever need anything, *anything,* you just give me a shout."

Leaning over, he kissed her cheek. "I never would've made it without you. Craig is going to need all the help he can get. Don't let him do anything I wouldn't do."

"Melody and I'll take good care of him."

"I know you will." Tears stung the back of his eyes, but he blinked them away. Pushing open the door, he stepped out. From the backseat of the car he pulled a small satchel and then stepped aside. Roseanne backed the car onto the main road. She waved once then drove back the way they had come.

Gideon faced the lane leading toward a large, rambling white house. Smoke rose from two of the home's three chimneys. Over the years, his family had added on to the original home with a second smaller house for his mother's parents.

The addition of a *Dawdi Haus,* or grandfather house, was a common practice among the Amish. Grandparents and elderly relatives were able to maintain their own households when they retired and yet were surrounded and included by their extended families. It was a good way to grow old.

A large well-tended barn and outbuildings stood a few dozen yards back from house. There were horses in the corral and cattle in the pasture. This was the home Gideon hadn't seen in ten years. From this spot nothing much had changed. Only everything had changed. He had changed.

Hefting his bag, he started walking up the road. The cold wind slipped under the collar of his coat, making him hunch his shoulders to block the breeze.

The snow on the ground crunched beneath his feet, making him think of his walk with Rebecca through the snow-covered streets of Hope Springs.

She wasn't the only reason he'd come back. Rebecca had merely been the needle on the compass pointing him to his way home. He hadn't realized how lost he truly was until he saw her again. Perhaps someday he would tell her she had been the instrument of his return.

In Gideon's mind, Booker no longer existed. His life in the English world was at an end. It was Booker who soared above the clouds and looked down on the backs of birds flying beneath him. It was plain Gideon Troyer walking this rural road with his feet planted firmly on the good earth God had made.

Even as Gideon faced the fact that he would never fly again, he wondered if he could do it. Could he gaze at the sky and not long to be up there? Giving up flying hurt as much as giving up an arm or a leg.

It wouldn't be easy to come back, but it was the right thing to do.

Plain Gideon had many tasks before him. The first was to gain his family's forgiveness. Facing his father and mother was shaping up to be a difficult thing as he approached the farmhouse. His heart started hammering. His palms grew sweaty. Admitting his mistake, making amends for the way he'd left, he had a lot to atone for. He prayed God would grant him the courage he needed this day.

When plain Gideon took his rightful place among the faithful, only then would he be free to discover if Rebecca Beachy still cared for him. If she did not, he would accept that it was God's will.

Please, Lord, give me the wisdom to convince her we belong together.

He arrived at the front door of his childhood home with a growing sense that he had finally made the right decision. This was where he was meant to be.

When the front door opened and his father walked out, Gideon's courage failed him. He couldn't speak.

His father's eyes widened in shock. "Gideon?"

Abraham Troyer had aged in the ten years that had passed. He seemed frail now. His shoulders bowed forward, as if the weight of his life was hard to carry. How much of the gray hair, how many of the worry lines on his face were due to Gideon's selfishness?

His father took a step toward. It broke the spell holding Gideon rooted to the spot. Dropping to one knee, Gideon bowed his head, closed his eyes and spoke the words that burned in his heart. "Father, forgive me, for I have sinned."

He heard a muffled gasp, but he was afraid to look up. What if too much time had passed? What if merely asking for forgiveness wasn't enough?

What could he do to convince his father that he was sincere?

Suddenly, he felt his father's hands drawing him to his feet. He opened his eyes and met his father's gaze. Tears rolled down his father's lean, leathery cheeks.

In a voice that shook, Abraham Troyer said, "*Mie, sohn,* you were forgiven the very day that you left. There is only rejoicing now that you have returned. *Gott* has answered my prayers. Praise be to Him."

Chapter Eight

Rebecca sat at her quilting frame stitching while Vera read to her from her siblings' letter that had arrived in the mail that morning. Each one of Rebecca's brothers and sisters added their pages to the letter and sent it on to the next in line so everyone could stay caught up on the family news. Rebecca, with Vera's help, would add her updates and send it on to her oldest sister to start the process all over again. Everyone except Grace. There were never any letters from her.

"Your brother William says his family is traveling to see your brother Leroy in Indiana after Christmas. He wants to know if you'd like to go along."

It had been four weeks since the auction and two weeks since Dr. White had started Rebecca on chemotherapy. Her surgery, scheduled for December twenty-first, was only three weeks away. By Christmas Eve she would know if her sight had been restored or not. Either way, it would be good to visit her brother. They hadn't seen each other for over a year.

"I look forward to going."

"Do you mean that?"

Vera's astonishment didn't surprise Rebecca. Vera knew Rebecca didn't like to travel. While her parents and siblings went often went to visit each other for extended stays, especially over Christmas, Rebecca rarely went along. She didn't like finding her way in new places.

"William says they'll leave the day after old Christmas."

Old Christmas was the Feast of the Epiphany, January sixth. "I will see if Samson Carter can drive me to William's home on that day. If he can't, I'll try to find another driver."

"I heard there is a new woman in town who drives Amish folks. Her name is Miriam Kauffman. She might be able to give you a ride if Samson is booked," Vera suggested.

"I will keep her name in mind. I can't believe how quickly Christmas is coming. We need to start baking. What else does William say?"

"He says the community is in turmoil because Gideon Troyer has come home."

Rebecca stabbed her finger with a needle. "Ouch!"

Her aunt asked, "What's wrong?"

Sucking her finger to ease the sting, Rebecca

used the moment to cover her shock. When she had her turbulent emotions under control, she said, "Gideon Troyer has come back? To stay?"

"That's what William says."

"Gideon's family must be overjoyed."

"I daresay they are, especially his mother. Imagine, returning to our faith after ten years in the outside world. It cannot be an easy thing. I wonder what brought him back."

Rebecca wondered the same thing. "Why is the community in turmoil?"

"According to your brother, there are some that don't believe he has truly repented."

"One of those would be Bishop Stoltzfus, I reckon." The bishop from her old community was distrustful of outsiders and ruled his flock with an iron hand, as she knew from unhappy personal experience.

"Weren't you sweet on the boy at one time?" her aunt asked.

Rebecca bent over her sewing again. "That was years ago."

"I remember your mother telling me the two of you were quite serious. That you might even marry."

"She was mistaken," Rebecca mumbled.

Gideon had come home. After all this time, it was hard to believe. What was he like now? Was he as handsome as she remembered? Was he still a bold, outspoken fellow who never took anything at face value? Unless he had changed a lot he would have a hard time reentering the Amish world.

In their youth, Gideon had often talked about leaving and about learning to fly. But after they were both baptized on the same September morning, she believed he had given up his outlandish plans.

If she had accepted his offer, would he have stayed among the faithful? For years she blamed herself for his leaving. Knowing how his parents suffered only made her feel worse.

"Then it was God's blessing that you didn't marry the boy. I wonder if he'll stay this time. I reckon all we can do is pray for him."

Gideon had been in Rebecca's prayers since the day of his departure. Why had he returned? "What else does my brother say?"

"Will says his boy David has come down with the mumps."

"He doesn't say anything else about Gideon?" Rebecca heard the rustle of paper as her aunt turned the page.

"No, he doesn't mention him again."

Rebecca had a hard time sorting out her feelings. Gideon had come back. On one hand she was happy for him and for his family, but on the other hand she worried for them. What if he couldn't adjust to living Amish after so many years away?

Vera finished the letter but Rebecca barely heard

a word. When she went home to visit her family it was possible she might run into Gideon. What would she say? Did she want to meet him again?

A flutter of nervousness caused her hand to shake as she tried to set her next stitch. Why were men always at the center of her distress? First it had been Gideon all those years ago, then Booker, and now Gideon again.

The sound of a horse and buggy pulling up outside caused Rebecca to set her stitching aside. "Are we expecting someone?"

"When Emma came by the other day, I asked if her husband could look at our washing machine. It's been making that funny noise again."

Adam Troyer was a handyman in the village as well as owner of the Wadler Inn with his wife. His prices were reasonable, and there were very few things he couldn't fix.

Rebecca asked, "Should I put on some *kaffi?*"

"That would be just the thing on such a cold day. Put out the peanut-butter cookies we made yesterday, too. I know for a fact that Adam likes them."

Rising from her chair, Rebecca made her way into the kitchen. At the sink, she filled their coffeepot with water until it touched her finger inside the rim. She opened the cupboard and pulled out the coffee can. After carefully filling the percolator basket with grounds, she carried the pot to the stove and put it on the back burner. After that, she opened a second cupboard and withdrew a plate.

The sound of the front door opening and a blast of cold air announced Adam's arrival. She said, "*Wilkumm,* have a seat, Adam, and the *kaffi* will be ready in no time. Do you take it black or with cream? I can't remember. *Aenti* Vera tells me you like peanut-butter cookies. You're in luck. I made some yesterday."

"*Danki,* Rebecca."

She moved along the counter, located the cookie jar and began piling cookies on the plate. She heard Adam clear his throat.

"I brought a helper today."

"Did you?" She added another handful of cookies and turned around.

Adam said, "You remember my cousin Gideon, don't you?"

"Hello, Rebecca."

The deep-timbered voice robbed her of coherent thought and made her knees go weak. The plate slipped from her numb fingers and crashed to the floor.

The stricken look on Rebecca's face cut Gideon to the quick. He knew this wouldn't be easy, but he wasn't expecting her to cringe at the sound of his voice.

She muttered, “I’m so sorry. That was careless of me.”

Vera rushed to help her. “Don’t worry, dear, it was an old dish, and I’m sure we have more cookies. Let me get it. I don’t want you to cut your hands on the broken glass. Stay where you are and I’ll get a broom.”

Adam grabbed Gideon’s sleeve. “Let’s take a look at that washing machine. We may not deserve cookies if we can’t get it fixed.”

Gideon hated to leave Rebecca standing in the kitchen looking mortified, but Adam gave him no choice. He led the way to a small back porch where an ancient wringer washer stood on rusting legs.

Looking from the wreck to his cousin, Gideon asked, “Are you sure you can fix this thing? It looks older than the hills.”

Adam chuckled. “They made things to last back in the day.”

“By back in the day I take it you mean 1925?”

“You’ve got a thing or two to learn if you’re going to work with me. This is a Maytag model E2L from 1969. It’s one of the best wringer washers ever made.”

Adam turned on the water and began filling the machine. Gideon blew on his bare hands. Even with the afternoon sun streaming in through the windows the room was frigid. “This is a cold place to do laundry. Why don’t they put the thing inside?”

"It was good enough for our mothers and grandmothers. We see no need to move the chore indoors."

"Is that your way of telling me I'm soft, cousin?"

"That's my way of reminding you that you must be careful how you speak."

Gideon adjusted the flat-topped black hat he wasn't yet accustomed to wearing. "How long did it take you?"

"To stop reaching for the nonexistent light switch every time I went into a dark room? About six months. I try to remind myself that it's not about electricity or cars or using buggies to get around. It's about living apart from a world that is filled with temptation and evil. Living a Plain life makes it easier to keep my mind on God and on His will. Not just every single day, but every hour of every single day."

"Not all of the outside world is evil."

"*Nee,* there is much *goot* in the hearts of men everywhere, but here, I find it is easier to be close to God."

"Do you ever regret coming back?"

"Every man faces temptations, Gideon. But when I see my wife's face each morning, I know this is where God wants me to be. If it is His will, I'll raise my children here and pray that they find the strength to stay among the people."

"I wish I had the strength of conviction you have."

"If you seek it with your whole heart it will be given to you."

When the washer tub was half full Adam turned off the water and turned on the machine. Instantly, they heard the strange noise Vera had reported.

Adam crossed his arms over his chest. "What are you thinking?"

"If this was a plane I wouldn't even taxi down the runway in it. The gears are slipping."

"I agree. Let's drain her, tip her over and get this motor apart."

Gideon flipped the switch that began to pump the water out a hose that drained to the backyard.

"When do you plan to tell her?" Adam asked as he unscrewed the cover.

"Tell who what?"

Adam shot Gideon a stern look. "When do you plan to tell Rebecca that you are Booker?"

Gideon couldn't meet his cousin's gaze. "Booker doesn't exist anymore."

"I doubt that will be the way Rebecca sees it. She believes Booker is responsible for making her surgery possible. Hand me that crescent wrench."

"It was one of the few good things he did with his life." Gideon laid the tool in Adam's outstretched hand.

Adam pointed to the wrench at Gideon's face. "You have no idea how grateful Rebecca and our entire community is for your gift."

"And that is exactly why I don't wish anyone to know it was me. I don't want the community's gratitude. I don't want Rebecca's gratitude. Can you understand that?" Gideon glanced toward the back door. This wasn't about money or status or acceptance. This was about helping Rebecca.

Adam shook his head. "I thought the point of you moving to Hope Springs was to pick up where you left off with Rebecca."

"The point of my coming here was to pick up where Gideon left off with Rebecca, not where Booker and Rebecca left off."

"I still think you're wrong. Secrets will come out."

"Hopefully, by the time that happens people will have formed their own opinions about me. I think they will understand that I didn't want to use my generosity to gain favor and I believe they will respect that."

"You mean you hope Rebecca will respect that."

"I'm not a fool, Adam. There's no guarantee that Rebecca will return my affections. I came back to my Amish heritage because I believe this is the life God wishes me to live. You, of all people, must understand that?"

"I do, for that is why I gave up the English world and returned to my family and my faith. I pray God will bless your decision. Ah, I believe I see what's wrong with this washer. Hand me my half-inch socket drive."

"Adam, have I thanked you for giving me a job and a place to stay?"

"About a hundred times. Let's see if I made the right decision. Hand me the crosshead screwdriver."

Twenty minutes later, Adam and Gideon were elbow-deep in motor parts when the back door opened. Vera stood there with her head cocked to the side. "Have you found the trouble?"

Rebecca came up behind Vera. "What's the verdict?"

Adam rose to his feet and held out a gear. "Your washer has a broken tooth, Vera. It's not something we can fix today. I'm going to have to take this piece to the shop and see if I can find a replacement for it. If I can't, perhaps Eli Imhoff can make a new one."

"Who is Eli?" Gideon asked. He forced himself to stay calm. So far Vera hadn't recognized him, but she could put two and two together at any minute. During the auction he'd been wearing his sunglasses and knit cap, but the night of the fire she would have seen his face clearly when she came to his room. That night he'd been hollow-eyed with several days' growth of beard on his cheeks and shaggy hair. He was clean-shaven now, and his mother had cut his hair in the traditional Amish style. Was there enough of a difference?

"Eli Imhoff is the local blacksmith," Adam replied.

Vera took the part from Adam's hand. "I've seen a

gear like this hanging in the barn. There are dozens of similar pieces out there. My *Onkel* Atlee, God rest his soul, never threw anything away."

Adam smiled at her. "If you have one that would be great. I could get your machine together today."

"Let me get my coat, and I will show you where he kept his things." Vera turned and went inside with Adam following close behind her. Gideon relaxed. It seemed Vera hadn't paid much attention to Booker during his time at the inn.

After Vera and Adam left, Gideon found himself alone with Rebecca. This was exactly where he had hoped to be. So why was he suddenly tongue-tied?

He gathered his courage. "Could we wait inside where it's warm?"

"Of course." Rebecca held the door open wider in invitation.

"Thanks. I mean, *danki*."

"Your Pennsylvania Dutch is rusty." She went ahead of him down the hall keeping one hand lightly in contact with the wall.

"I'm sure it will come back to me." Did she recognize his voice now that his illness had healed? Did she suspect he was the man she knew as Booker? He longed to tell her, but he wasn't Booker anymore. He'd left that life behind. He wanted her to know the man he was intent on becoming.

When they reached the kitchen she moved to the

far side of the table and faced him. "Are you ready for coffee and cookies now?"

"Have you picked all the glass shards out of them?"

"All that I could see." A smile twitched at the corner of her mouth.

"Blind humor. Are you trying to put me at ease?"

"Why would you be ill at ease?"

Because I left you. Because I spent ten years excommunicated from the church and nobody believes I intend to stay now.

Instead of baring his soul, he took a seat at the table. "I have not spent much time with the sight-impaired. Feel free to correct me if I say something stupid."

She pulled a pair of mugs from the cabinet beside the sink and carried them to the stove. He watched her fill them just to the brim and wondered how she managed a task he couldn't do with his eyes closed.

Finally, his curiosity won out. "How can you do that without spilling any?"

She stiffened. "Practice."

"This is where you tell me that was a stupid question."

"Your question is not stupid. I've had years to learn how to do almost everything a sighted person can do. I simply do things differently."

"I'm impressed by your skills."

She carried the mugs to the table. "My skill at dropping plates?"

"Something tells me you don't do that often. I'm sorry if my unannounced arrival was a shock."

"I learned of your return to Berlin in a letter that arrived from my brother this morning, but I didn't expect you to show up in my kitchen a few minutes later."

"Did your brother pass on the juicy details of my trouble with Bishop Stoltzfus?" It was hard to keep that bitterness out of his voice. It had taken more courage than he thought he possessed to beg forgiveness from his bishop. When the man announced he didn't believe Gideon was sincere, it caused quite a stir and a division in the church.

"William didn't mention any details. Your family must have been overjoyed when you came back."

He nodded his head and then realized she couldn't see that. "My mother kept hugging me. She cried all day. When I told her to stop being sad, she said they were tears of joy and could not be stemmed."

"I'm sure she meant it."

"My youngest brother wasn't quite so demonstrative."

"He wasn't happy at your return?"

"Let's just say Joseph has reservations about whether or not I will stay." Along with the bishop and half of his family's congregation.

She rolled her cup between her palms. "I'm sorry, but can you blame him?"

"Not really." It was hard to read her expression. Did she doubt his resolve in returning, too? How could she not? *He* wasn't sure if he could stay.

Propping her elbows on the table, she said, "Time will give him the answer. Is that why you aren't staying with them?"

"My mother thought it best if I spend some time with Adam, being as he spent a long time in the English world and came back to stay."

She folded her arms across her chest. She had yet to take a sip of her coffee. It was clear she was struggling to be cordial.

He said, "I know it was a shock to you when I left the way I did."

"You were never content with our slow Amish ways. I remember you as a wild, defiant boy."

"And I remember you as a sweet-natured girl who forgave all my indiscretions. We had some fine times together during our rumspringa."

Her face grew pale. She folded her arms tightly across her chest. "*Ja,* fine times."

"I was sorry to learn about your affliction. Adam told me the community has raised enough money for you to have surgery."

"I don't think of it as an affliction. It's just the way my life is. The surgery's chances of success are only fifty-fifty. I'm trying not to get my hopes up.

I am happy here with my *aenti.* I have nieces and nephews who come to visit, so I am not lonely. I still have my quilting, and I enjoy that immensely."

"That's good."

She finally took a sip of her coffee and he took a drink of his. The silence stretched out between them.

"I hope Adam can fix our washer. I know Vera doesn't want to have to buy a new one."

"I hear he's a pretty good handyman."

"*Ja,* people say so." She nervously raised the cup to her lips again.

This small talk wasn't what he wanted. He wanted to start over with her. Earn her trust. Win her love. And he had absolutely no idea how to do that.

Rebecca wasn't sure how much longer she could sit and pretend that Gideon Troyer was a normal visitor. Her heart was hammering. Her hands were shaking. She wanted him to leave. Even though she was the one who turned down his offer of marriage, she never gave up loving him. When he left it was as if he took a piece of her heart with him.

Now that scar on her heart was open and bleeding again.

She rose from her chair, knocking against the table in her haste. She heard the cups rattle but she didn't care if they spilled. "Vera and Adam have been gone a long time. Perhaps you should see if you can help."

"Rebecca, can you forgive me?"

She had sent him away. When the darkness descended over her life it wasn't his fault he wasn't there to hold her and comfort her. And yet it was his fault. If his faith had been strong, he would have been there for her.

She spoke the words her Amish teaching required her to say. "Of course I forgive you. I forgave you a long time ago."

"Thank you, Rebecca. It means the world to me."

The sound of the outside door opening saved her from having to reply. When Vera and Adam returned, Rebecca excused herself and rushed up the stairs to her bedroom.

She closed the door and leaned against it. Angry tears stung her eyes. Wiping at them with fierce swipes, she vowed they would be the last tears she shed over Gideon Troyer.

Up until a month ago, her life had a simple rhythm. Gardening in the spring and summer, canning in the fall and quilting over the long winter days. It didn't matter that she couldn't see the fresh greenness of the spring. She could smell it in the air and feel the warmth of the sun on her face. It didn't matter that she couldn't watch the snow fall. She knew when it fell by the silence that blanketed the land. It was enough for her to work and feel the seasons passing by, for they defined her life.

Then, a few short weeks ago, she met a man who touched her soul the way only one man had before. That he was forbidden to her was as painful as holding someone else's child and knowing she would never hold her own babe. The day she gave him her quilt was the first time in her life she questioned her decision to stay among the Amish.

The morning after he left, she woke knowing he had been the test—and she passed. If she never regained her vision, her faith was strong enough to sustain that disappointment. Contentment had entered her soul.

Now Gideon was back and her heart was being torn once more. All her old feelings for him came rushing back to life at the sound of his voice.

Why now? Why, after so many years of darkness and bitterness overcome, was she being tested again?

"Haven't I suffered enough, Lord? Haven't I paid long enough for my sin?"

Chapter Nine

Gideon arrived at Rebecca's home the following afternoon with the needed part in his pocket. In spite of all the parts in Vera's barn, Adam couldn't find the right one. Yesterday hadn't gone as well as Gideon hoped. Instead of being thrilled to see him, Rebecca had looked terrified. Hopefully, once the shock of his arrival wore off she would remember how close they had been.

As he climbed out of Adam's buggy, he noticed the sounds of several wind chimes around the property. He'd been too nervous to notice them yesterday. He wondered if it was Vera or Rebecca who enjoyed the musical notes.

To his relief, Rebecca answered the door when he knocked. He'd been half afraid she would be hiding in her room or gone. "Good afternoon, Rebecca. It's Gideon. I have come to finish the work on your washing machine."

"I've been expecting you. My aunt will be back shortly. She took a kettle of soup to a neighbor who has been ill." She stepped back to let him enter.

He stomped his feet to rid his boots of the clinging snow and entered the kitchen with his toolbox in hand. The smell of cooking apples filled the air.

She said, "I'm sure you remember where the washer is. I will let you find your own way." Her nonchalant tone took him aback. She went to the stove, picked up a ladle and began stirring the contents of a large pan.

Again, not the reaction he had hoped for. He said, "Something sure smells good."

"Pie filling."

When she didn't elaborate he searched his mind for something to breech the growing chasm he sensed between them. "As I recall, you were a pretty good cook."

She laid the ladle down. "I don't recollect that you were interested in my housewifely skills."

"True. I was more about finding ways to sneak a kiss from you than trying out your cooking." He waited for her response.

Turning around, she crossed her arms over her chest. "*Ja,* that is the way I remember you—as a shallow fellow often up to no good."

Definitely not the reaction he was hoping for. "That about sums up my misspent youth. Fortunately, I grew up."

"Better late than never." She turned back to the stove, but he noticed her hand wasn't quite steady as she put the lid on the kettle.

Accepting his dismissal with a heavy heart, Gideon went out to the rear porch and began reassembling her washing machine. He took his time, making sure the new piece fit perfectly, then he fired up the gas motor and began filling the machine.

When it looked as if everything was going to work, he stuck his head inside the back door. "Rebecca, do you have some clothes to be washed? I want to run a cycle and make sure the drum empties as it should and I don't want to waste all the water."

She came to the hallway, but didn't come toward him. "I have baking to do. The laundry can wait."

"I know it can, but why should it? Let me get one load out of your way."

"Laundry is woman's work."

"Unless a man is unmarried, then he must learn to do his own."

She hesitated, but finally nodded once. "We have several loads, but they aren't sorted."

"I promise not to mix whites and colors."

"I doubt you used a wringer washer where you lived before."

"No, but I remember helping my mother with her laundry chores. I think I can manage."

"Very well. I will get the hamper."

She entered a room partway down the hall and came out a few seconds later with a tall, woven wood clothes basket. "My aunt will be grateful to have her work cut in half before washday. Don't add too much soap."

"No problem." He took the burden from her and returned to the machine. She stood for a moment as if she wanted to say something more, but in the end, she went inside without another comment.

He found the laundry detergent inside a cabinet hanging on the wall. After adding the recommended amount to the tub, he followed with a dozen dresses and aprons in assorted colors of blue. The old washer chugged along without missing a beat. Glancing up, he happened to notice a reflection in the porch window. Rebecca stood just inside the door listening to him.

He started to hum while he worked, a German hymn, a song he knew Rebecca liked when they were young. She had a sweet voice and often led the girls during the youth singings they had attended. Memories of the tame gatherings he'd found boring as a teenager now ranked among the highlights of his time with Rebecca.

When the wash cycle was done, he fed the clothes through the wringer and into the rinse tub. After letting them soak a few minutes, he stirred them with a wooden stick he found propped in the corner, and then fed them back through the wringer again.

He piled the wet clothes on a Formica-topped table beside the back door.

He stopped humming and said as if to himself, "If I were Vera's clothespins, where would I be hiding?" He started opening cabinets.

After a second, Rebecca stepped through the doorway. Her expression had softened. "They are out on the clothesline post in a clothespin bag."

"I would have found them." He tried to sound defensive, but he was smiling.

"Maybe you would. Maybe not."

He didn't want to break the thin thread of friendliness he saw forming between them. "The machine seems to be working fine. Eli Imhoff made a perfect replacement for the gear."

"You must thank him for us."

"I will. I'll see him at church services on Sunday." He hoped his statement made it clear he was returning to his Amish faith, not just paying it lip service.

He walked out the porch door to the clothesline reel hanging off the side of the house. Over the doorway, he noticed another small set of brass wind chimes clinking in the breeze. After pulling the retractable line from the side of the house, he stretched it to a T-post in the center of the yard and fastened it.

Setting the basket of clothes carefully in the snow, he began to hang them up, humming again as he did. This time he chose an English hymn with a familiar tune although he couldn't recall the exact words of the song.

He had five dresses pinned to the line before she ventured out the door. She stopped a few feet away from him with her arms crossed against the cold. "'Amazing Grace' has always been one of my favorites."

"I'm a bit rusty on the words. How does it go?"

She sang the opening lines. "'Amazing Grace, how sweet the sound, that saved a wretch like me. I once was lost but now am found, was blind, but now I see.'"

He could have kicked himself. He stammered, "I didn't mean to… That was thoughtless of me. Forgive me."

She arched one eyebrow. "Gideon, I don't need the lyrics of a song to remind me that I'm blind."

"No, I guess not." From friend to fool in three seconds flat. Maybe he didn't deserve to win her heart.

He might be able to accept that if he didn't care for her so deeply.

"It's still one of my favorite hymns," she insisted.

He relaxed when he realized she wasn't upset. "You should go back in the house before you catch your death. You don't even have a coat on."

"Don't forget to empty the water from the washer

tub. I don't want to find a giant ice cube in it the next time I need to use it."

"I'll take care of it. Don't worry," he assured her.

She cocked her head to the side slightly, as if listening, then she turned around and headed straight toward the back door. He realized the wind chimes were a means to help her find her way.

She opened the porch door, but paused. "You weren't shallow and always up to no good when we were young. I shouldn't have said that."

Before he could reply, she went inside. Gideon watched her disappear into the house and seeds of happiness sprouted in his heart. Things might be looking up for him, after all.

Inside the house, Rebecca moved her pie filling off the stove and set it to cooling on the counter. Nervous butterflies churned in her stomach. She felt like a teenager waiting to sneak out of her first date. Gideon Troyer was back.

She had spent a sleepless night building up her defenses against the charm he possessed. A lot of good it had done.

Hearing him stutter an apology for reminding her that she was blind made her remember the little boy she used to know. The boy who had gotten in trouble in the third grade for cutting the ribbons off her *kapp.* The boy who dared her to ride standing up on the back of her papa's plow horse and bore the brunt of her father's displeasure when she fell off and sprained her ankle.

Gideon had charmed her from the age of eight. Why did she think it would be different now?

She heard the back door open and close and then his footsteps coming up the hallway. If he would be living in Hope Springs she would have to accustom herself to meeting him now and again. They had been friends long before they became starry-eyed teenagers in love with the idea of being in love.

"Have you anything else that needs fixing?" he asked.

Could he fix an old broken heart? Where would he find the parts for that?

"*Nee,* I don't believe we do. Would you like some coffee before you go?"

"I would. Will you be making one of your pies soon?" She heard the smile in his voice and smiled back.

"I'll be making apple strudel soon."

"Sounds great. What can I do to help?"

"Stay out of my way and enjoy your coffee."

"Bossy as ever, aren't you?"

She rose to his bait. "I was never bossy."

"Yes, you were."

"Do you want strudel or not?" she demanded with mock severity.

"You've always had a wonderful personality, a giving nature, a sweet temper."

"That's better."

"Was that good enough for hot strudel with maybe a touch of cream?"

She chuckled. *"Ja."*

"Wunderbaar!"

"See, it is always better to tell the truth, Gideon. The truth earns its own reward."

A warm glow of satisfaction settled in the middle of her chest. She would hold fast to their friendship. Perhaps in time, she would even learn to let go of the love that was never meant to be.

The sound of the front door opening signaled her aunt's return. Vera came into the kitchen along with a gust of cold winter wind. "I believe we are going to get more snow. Hello, Gideon. I see by the clothes on the line that my washer has been repaired. Rebecca, I told you not to worry about getting the wash done."

"It was not me. It was Gideon who did your laundry."

"I only did one load to make sure the machine was working correctly," he said.

"Perhaps I should take out a piece of the motor before every wash day and call you to come out and fix it."

"Then the price of my service call will go up sharply," he said with a chuckle.

"How is Mr. Pater?" Rebecca asked. When Vera learned their English neighbor was suffering from a bad chest cold, she started taking soup to him each day.

"He is much better today. Gideon, how is your family?" Vera asked.

"As far as I know they are all well."

Vera pulled out a chair and took a seat at the table. "What a wonderful time you must have had getting to know them and their spouses."

He said, "I still have trouble telling Levi's *kinders* apart. They all look like their father did when he was a child."

Rebecca listened with delight to his account of meeting his newest family members. She could hear the happiness beneath his words as clearly as she heard the wind chimes that hung from the rear of the house. She put her pan of strudel in the oven and set the windup timer for twenty minutes.

Gideon said, "Catch me up on your family, Rebecca. I know you said you have nieces and nephews. Which of your brothers and sisters have children of their own?"

"They all have children," Rebecca replied. A tang of regret touched her but she brushed it aside. She was happy for every one of her siblings.

"Who did Grace marry?" Gideon asked. "I remember the way she tormented my brother Levi. She liked him—she didn't like him—she liked him again. It drove him crazy."

Rebecca froze. He didn't know. No one had told him.

He must have seen her distress because he asked, "Did I say something wrong?"

She folded her arms across her middle. "Grace isn't with us anymore."

"She died? How?" he asked, shock clear in his voice.

Vera said quietly, "She isn't dead, but we no longer mention her name."

Rebecca bit her lip and remained silent. The disgrace should have been hers, not her sister's.

On Sunday, Rebecca rode in silence beside her aunt in their buggy as they traveled the ten miles to an outlying farm for the preaching service. Even with the curtains tied down and quilts on their laps it was chilly inside the buggy. The bricks they had heated to keep their feet warm on the journey were growing cool by the time they reached their destination.

During the long ride she had plenty of time to think about Gideon's visit the day before. Far from being as awkward as she imagined it would be, Gideon's company had felt comfortable.

"We must be among the last to arrive judging by

the number of buggies here," Vera commented as she drew their horse to a stop.

The door opened and a young man's voice greeted them. It was one of the farmer's sons. "I will take care of your horse."

"Danki," Vera replied. "There is grain for her in the back."

Leaving the buggy, Rebecca wondered if Gideon was there before them. She wanted to ask, but she didn't. Knowing her aunt, she would soon have the details on everyone in attendance. Vera's love of gossip was well known.

"Now that is odd," Vera said with a lowered voice.

"What?" Rebecca prompted, waiting for more of an explanation.

"There is an English woman here. That must be Ada Kauffman's English daughter. I see the resemblance. She's the one I told you who offers taxi service."

Rebecca was more interested in finding out if Gideon had arrived. She knew he was staying with Adam and Emma so she asked, "Do you see Emma? I hope her pregnancy is going well."

"Yes, she is chatting with Katie Sutter, Faith Lapp and Karen Imhoff. Emma has that glow about her. Pregnancy certainly agrees with her."

"I wonder if Adam feels the same way. Do you see him?"

"*Ja,* he's looking more like a proud papa now that he has some chin hair. His cousin is with him."

"His cousin? Oh, you mean Gideon." She tried to sound barely interested, but she could feel her aunt's gaze boring into her.

"He's looking this way."

Rebecca perked up. "Is he?"

"He is indeed, and so is Daniel Hershberger. He's coming our way. The man is interested in you, mark my words."

"Gideon? That's ridiculous."

"No, silly. Daniel."

"*Guder mariye,* Rebecca." Daniel's booming voice filled the farmyard.

"*Guder mariye,* Daniel," Rebecca replied in a soft tone, hoping he would take the hint and lower his voice. It was a foolish hope.

"I thought what a beautiful day this is, but it is much brighter now that you are here."

Rebecca lowered her voice further. "You should not say such a thing."

"A modest woman is a man's true treasure." He wasn't shouting, but he might as well have been. The hum of conversations around them died away.

Rebecca pasted a smile on her face and pinched her aunt's arm. "Isn't it time we went inside?"

"If you wish. Daniel, we will see you later."

"I look forward to speaking with you and your

niece again. I must go tell Reuben I'm waiting for a rematch on our checkers game."

Rebecca had endured one long, tedious evening with Daniel at her grandfather's home a week after the fire. She would avoid a repeat if it were possible. How could she have entertained the idea of marriage to the man?

As she took her place beside her aunt on the women's side of the wooden benches lined up inside the farmhouse, she wondered if Gideon had overheard Daniel's compliments to her. Although it was vain, some small part of her hoped that he had.

Gideon joined Adam and his friends in the airy barn following the three-hour-long service. Bishop Zook was a gifted preacher, clearly inspired by God to bring the Lord's words to his flock. Up at the house, the benches were being rearranged to make seating for the congregation to share a midday meal. Because the elders would eat first, the younger members amused themselves with games or visiting while they waited their turns.

Gideon stood among the men and saw a few faces from the night of the fire around him. He wondered if any of them recognized him from his time in Hope Springs as Booker. If they did, no one mentioned it. Perhaps they were willing to accept him for who he was now and not for who he'd been. He prayed it was so.

"How are you adjusting to Amish life again?" Jonathan Dressler asked. Beside him, fifteen-year-old Jacob Imhoff was trying to look as if he belonged in this group of men twice his age.

Gideon folded his arms over his chest. "I will admit it's tough sometimes. How are you doing? English to Amish, that's a rare move. Not many can accept our ways. At least I knew what I was getting into when I came back."

"I miss my computer," Jonathan answered with a grin.

"I think I miss having my pickup the most," Adam said, a tinge of wistfulness in his voice.

"Is it true you were a pilot?" Jacob focused his awe-filled gaze on Gideon. "I can't believe you don't miss flying."

"I do, but I try not to dwell on it." That didn't always work. He missed the freedom of the air, but he was striving to find contentment on the ground.

"What he needs is an Amish wife to take his mind off his English ways," Adam suggested with a chuckle. "It worked for me."

Jonathan nudged Gideon and tipped his head toward the young women grouped together across the way. "See one you like?"

Gideon accepted their good-natured ribbing and pretended to look over the women. "Jacob, your sister is single, isn't she?"

"*Nee,* she will soon be taken." Jonathan's sharp reply set Adam, Gideon and Jacob to laughing.

Adam stroked his beard. "The bishop's oldest daughter is of age."

The men looked toward the bishop's hawk-faced wife, then looked at each other. They all shook their heads. "Not a chance," Gideon said.

His new friends continued to suggest possible mates, but no one brought up Rebecca's name. Finally, he couldn't keep silent any longer. "Rebecca Beachy is still single. She's not a youngster, but she's not too old. We're the same age."

Jacob frowned. "She's pretty enough, but she is blind."

"That doesn't mean she can't be a wife and mother. Adam, do you know what became of her sister Grace?"

Adam shrugged. "She left the Amish, that's all I know."

"Rebecca said her family doesn't speak of her anymore. I wondered why." It was the change in Rebecca's expression at the mention of her sister that had piqued his interest. He'd never seen such sadness on her face.

Eli Imhoff joined their group. "Gideon, how did my washer part work out?"

"It fit like a glove," Gideon assured him.

Jacob spoke up. "Papa, we were trying to find a woman for Gideon. Any suggestions?"

"Find a woman who can cook," Eli stated firmly. "Looks fade, cooking doesn't."

"Rebecca is a good cook." Gideon was happy to list her accomplishments. He didn't like that she had been overlooked in her own community.

"There are plenty of healthy women to choose from around here. A man needs a strong wife to stand by his side," Jacob insisted with all the assurance of a teenager who had yet to go on his first date.

Gideon glanced toward the house and saw Rebecca come out with her aunt. He said, "What a man needs most is a woman who loves him."

The problem he faced was how to convince Rebecca that they were meant for each other. When he looked her way again, he saw her grandfather standing at her side. Reuben was staring straight at Gideon.

Chapter Ten

"Emma, Gideon is desperately in need of your help."

Gideon caught Adam's cheeky grin and wanted nothing more than to stuff a sock in his cousin's big mouth. Muttering under his breath, Gideon said, "See if I confide in you again."

The two men were stacking chairs on tables in the café in preparation for cleaning the floors after closing. Outside the windows, the street of the town blinked with Christmas cheer as the townspeople and businessmen turned on their holiday lights.

"What help can I give, Gideon?" Emma asked. She was sweeping beneath the tables and booths.

"Never mind," he said quickly.

"My cousin wants to court a woman and he has forgotten how we Amish do it." Adam chuckled with glee as he ducked Gideon's halfhearted punch.

"Adam, stop teasing Gideon." Her stern tone

made both men look in her direction. She leveled a no-nonsense glare at her spouse.

Adam wasn't the least bit intimidated. He grinned at her and said, "I'll go fill the sugar dispensers."

He took the tray of glass containers and carried them into the kitchen. When he was out of sight, Emma turned to Gideon. "Pay no attention to your cousin. He loves to tease. Who is this special woman?"

"I'd rather not say. Courting was much easier when I was young."

"You are not so very old."

"Maybe not, but I'm too old to attend the singings and such. I can't ask her to a movie. I'm at a loss."

"There are many ways for you to get together. You can take her to visit her family. You can take her on a buggy or sleigh ride, just the two of you some evening. You can bring her here for a meal. Every woman likes a break from cooking."

"I've already thought of those things, but I'm not sure they set the right tone."

Emma tilted her head to the side. "Isn't showing her you want to spend time together the right tone?"

"The thing is, I'm afraid she'll say no if I come straight out and ask her to dinner or to go for a sleigh ride. I want her to get to know me better, but in a friendly way. I want her to feel comfortable in my company."

"You are new to our church. Well, perhaps we

could get up an ice-skating party and make sure she is invited."

"I'm pretty sure she won't skate."

Emma laid her broom aside and planted her hands on her hips. "I could make more useful suggestions if I knew who I was talking about."

Gideon knew Emma and Rebecca were friends. He took a second to wonder what Emma would think about him courting her friend. After all, how could Emma be certain he would remain Amish? He knew a lot of people had their doubts. Unless he found a few dozen things to repair in Rebecca's house he didn't have an excuse to spend much time in her company.

If he could convince Rebecca of his feelings before she had her surgery, he could be by her side no matter what her results were. He needed her to understand his affection had nothing to do with her sight or lack of it. He decided to take this chance.

Drawing a deep breath, he said, "It's Rebecca Beachy."

Emma's brows arched in surprise. "You wish to court Rebecca? You don't mind that she is blind?"

"Why should I mind? She is funny, she is devout, she is hard-working and she has a wonderful smile. I loved her when we were young. I never thought I'd have a chance to love her again, but God has been good to me. After all these years she is not married and beyond my reach. Rebecca is the woman of my heart."

Smiling broadly, Emma said, "Rebecca enjoys ice-skating."

It was his turn to be stunned. "She does?"

"Have you solved my cousin's woes?" Adam asked as he brought the filled sugar containers back from the kitchen.

Emma winked at Gideon. "*Nee,* but we have decided to have a skating party this coming weekend. Do you think Elam Sutter will let us use his pond?"

Adam plunked down his tray on the table beside her. "No harm in asking. It sounds like right *goot* fun."

Laying a finger on her lips, Emma tapped them slowly. "I will make up a picnic basket and bake some pies. We may even close the café so the girls who work for us can come."

Adam grinned. "She will let our English guests starve. It does not matter that they pay the bills."

"Nonsense. I will make sure there is plenty of bread and meat for sandwiches on the sideboard."

She started sweeping again. "This is a *goot* idea if I do say so myself."

Gideon didn't care whose idea it was as long as Rebecca was there.

Emma stopped what she was doing. "Gideon, I almost forgot. Reuben Beachy came in today. He wanted me to tell you he has a used leather-cutting machine being delivered next week and he wants you to make some repairs on it."

A shiver of unease slipped down Gideon's spine. "He asked for me, not for Adam?"

Smiling brightly, Emma nodded. "*Ja.* He said giving you the job was his way of helping you get started in the business community. He is a fine man."

Adam glanced at Gideon and his smile disappeared. "He's a fine man and very sharp for his age. Do not assume otherwise."

"A skating party. What a wonderful idea. I'm so excited." Katie Sutter clapped her hands together. Her two-year-old daughter, Rachel, playing on the floor at her feet, clapped, too, making all the women smile.

"What do you think, Rebecca?" Emma asked as they sat together around the kitchen table in the home of Faith and Adrian Lapp.

"I think it sounds like fun." Rebecca held a skein of yarn open on her hands as Faith unwound it. Katie, Emma and Sarah were cutting pieces of fabric remnants and sorting them in preparation for Rebecca's next quilting project. Since Rebecca didn't feel comfortable attacking pieces of cloth with scissors, she was helping Faith with her knitting.

"We can have a bonfire and roast hot dogs. I love

doing that. Elam is going to make sure we have plenty of benches to sit on, too. I can't wait until Saturday." Katie's enthusiasm was catching and her friends were happy to indulge her.

Katie's childhood, under the thumb of her cruel older brother, had been bereft of childish fun. Elam, her doting husband, was happy to help her make wonderful new memories for her and their children.

Faith said, "I don't skate, but I can't wait to see Kyle learn. He'll enjoy it for sure."

Rebecca heard the door bang open and suspected the culprit was Faith's nephew. When she heard his voice she knew she had guessed correctly. "*Mamm,* Myrtle spit on *Daed* and me again."

A sour smell permeated the room as heavy footsteps followed Kyle's into the kitchen. Adrian's deep voice said, "Faith, I know you love that alpaca, but she is going to find her long scrawny neck tied in a bow one of these days."

Everyone giggled for there wasn't an ounce of malice in his words. Faith sighed, rose to her feet and handed her half-wound ball of yarn to Rebecca. "I'll be the one tying the knot because I'm the one doing the extra laundry. There are clean shirts in the bedroom. Take those off and let me soak them."

As they trooped out of the room, Sarah whispered, "Did you notice Kyle is calling them *Mamm* and *Daed,* now? I knew he would be happy here, but I never expected to see my cousin Adrian so happy again after his first wife and child perished. God was good to bring Faith and Kyle into his life."

Katie said, "Kyle has adjusted well to our Amish ways. To look at him you would never know he was raised in an English home."

"I know someone else who is adjusting well to our Amish ways," Emma added.

"Are you talking about Jonathan?" Katie asked. "It's hard to believe he has been with us for a year now. Elam tells me he plans to be baptized soon."

Emma said, "I was talking about Gideon Troyer."

Rebecca kept her voice level. "He has not been with us long. He may fall back into his old ways. If a man breaks his vow once, he may do it again."

"Do you really think so?" It was Katie's voice this time.

Emma was quick to speak up for Gideon. "I believe he is sincere."

"What did I miss?" Faith asked as she came back into the room. She went to the sink and began filling it with water. The smell of lemon-scented laundry detergent quickly overpowered the stink of alpaca spit.

Emma said, "We were talking about Gideon Troyer. I said I think he is sincere in his desire to live Amish."

"That's because you love Adam and he returned from the outside world," Rebecca pointed out.

Faith began swishing the shirts in the water. "I

agree with Emma. I see a man who wants to live Plain. If I didn't, I wouldn't have rented my old house to him."

Rebecca perked up. "Gideon has rented a house?" That did sound as if he intended to stay a while.

"*Ja.* Adrian and I didn't want it to sit vacant, but we didn't want to sell it. We would like Kyle to live there when he is grown, but the place needs many repairs. Gideon said he would do them in exchange for a lower rent. It was an excellent solution so we agreed. I believe Gideon's mind is made up. I think he is here to stay."

Rebecca wished she could be as certain. "Time will give us the answer."

"It's no easy thing to give up the English life," Katie said quietly.

"You did it," Sarah pointed out. Everyone knew Katie had followed her English boyfriend into the outside world and only returned to Hope Springs after he left her pregnant and destitute. With no place to go, she had returned to her brother's house to beg his forgiveness only to find he and his wife had moved away.

"If it had not been for the kindness of Elam and his mother I would have gone back. We must all show Gideon that he has made the right choice."

"How do we do that?" Rebecca asked.

"Do what Elam and Nettie did for me. Treat Gideon with kindness and forgiveness. Treat him like he has always been, and will always be, one of us. If we doubt him we show him our own lack of faith."

Rebecca nodded. They were wise words and she held them in her heart. She wanted to believe Gideon would stay more than she cared to admit, but did she dare?

Gideon was stunned to see a passenger van pull up and stop in front of his new home Friday afternoon. He was even more shocked to see the doors open and members of his family begin climbing out.

He moved toward them. "What is this? Why didn't you tell me you were coming?"

"Then it wouldn't have been a surprise," his mother announced as Abraham helped her out of the van. Behind his parents came Levi and his young wife, Mary, carrying a baby in her arms and followed by three stair-step blond boys in identical black hats like the one their father wore.

From the far side of the vehicle came his sisters, Betty and Susie. Each of them had toddlers in tow. They both greeted Gideon with a quick peck on the cheek. Joseph was the last one out of the vehicle. He hung back from the others.

Gideon's father looked the house over. "Is the roof sound?"

His father, although primarily a farmer, had worked odd jobs in construction for as long as

Gideon could remember. "As near as I can tell it is, but I would value a second opinion."

"I will take a look. Have you a ladder?" Abraham asked.

Gideon nodded. "*Ja,* it's leaning against the back porch."

Waneta motioned to Joseph who was watching Levi unload boxes and baskets from the back of the van. "Joseph, go with your father and make sure the he doesn't fall off the roof."

"Have Gideon go. He isn't afraid of heights," Joseph countered.

Waneta gave him a stern look. "Neither are you and I want to speak to Gideon."

She and the women bustled up the steps and into the house. Levi brought a large box and pushed it into Gideon's hands. "I will go help *Daed.* You can unload the van."

Levi glanced after their mother and said, "I hope you have a ready list of eligible women in the area for *Mamm.* I think you're about to get the, 'It takes a good woman to make a good home' speech. If you don't, I'll bake you a pie."

Gideon inclined his head closer to Levi. "I don't have a long list. I have one name. Is the speech true?"

Levi smiled fondly at his boys. "*Ja.* It's true. But as happy as you will be with a wife, just wait till the babies arrive."

Talk of marriage and babies could wait. For now, Gideon was overjoyed to have his family around him. After ten long years of solitude, he was part of something bigger, something wonderful once again. He was part of the Troyer family.

He looked down at Levi's boys, standing quiet and patient beside their papa. He said, "How would you boys like to see some very strange animals?"

The youngsters looked at Levi. He nodded. "You may go with your *Onkel* Gideon."

Gideon gave Levi back the box and said, "Put it in the kitchen and tell the women I'll be back in a few minutes."

"What kind of animals?" the oldest one asked. He reached up to take Gideon's hand.

A thrill of happiness shot through Gideon as he grasped the small fingers. Smiling, he said, "The woman who owns this place raises alpacas. They are out in the orchard."

"What's an almapa?" the second youngest asked.

Joseph answered, "An alpaca is like a camel. Are they mean?"

Gideon looked at Joseph and saw the light of interest in his eyes. Pleased, Gideon said, "Some of them spit."

Joseph came toward Gideon and picked up the youngest child. Holding the two-year-old, Joseph spoke to him. "We can spit back, right, Melvin?"

The toddler nodded. “Me ’pit.” He proceeded to demonstrate his skill.

Gideon laughed. “Maybe I should warn the herd that Melvin is on the way.”

Joseph adjusted the child’s hat. “The barn cats at home give him a wide berth.”

Walking toward the orchard, Gideon was filled with a deep sense of contentment. In the future his children would play with these cousins. They would gather together at his parents’ farm for holidays, weddings and birthdays. He would never be excluded again.

The skating party was well under way on Saturday when Gideon, along with Adam and Emma, arrived at the Sutter farm. After helping Emma down from the buggy, Gideon unhitched their horse and led him to the corral where several dozen horses were tied up along the fence. Still in their harnesses, the animals munched contentedly on the hay spread out at their feet and waited for their owners to claim them when they were ready to go home.

Gideon met up with Adam and Emma again. Taking one of the baskets Emma had packed with goodies from her arm, Gideon walked behind them as they followed a trampled path to a large pond at the base of the hill. A bonfire burned in a flattened area two dozen feet from the edge of the pond.

There were at least twenty adults and twice that many children already skating.

"Emma, I'm so glad you could make it." Katie Sutter waved at them from a makeshift table loaded down with food.

Gideon handed over his basket and looked around for Rebecca. She wasn't among the women around the table, nor was she sitting on the wooden benches Elam Sutter had supplied for spectators and tired skaters. The party had seemed like a good idea when Emma suggested it, but if Rebecca didn't come he was back to square one.

Emma moved to stand beside him. "She's already out on the ice. Get your skates on."

He looked at the crowd of people circling the pond and spotted her skating beside a young woman. Rebecca held on to her partner's hand but she skated with ease, occasionally turning to glide backward. He gazed at her in amazement.

"Get your skates on," Emma prompted again. "I'm sure Sally would like a chance to skate with some of the young fellows here. I know several who are eager to offer."

Gideon didn't need to be told twice. He took a seat on one of the nearby benches and traded his boots for a pair of skates he had borrowed from Adam. After lacing them up, he took a few uncertain steps out onto the ice.

He didn't fall, but he came close. It had been a

few years since he last ventured onto a frozen pond. His confidence grew quickly as his skills returned. When he was sure he wouldn't make a fool of himself, he skated toward Rebecca.

Reaching her side, he said, "You continue to amaze me, Rebecca."

"Do I?" Her smile was bright and her cheeks flushed pink from the cold and her exertion.

"Would you mind if I made a round or two with you?" He held his breath as he waited for her reply.

The young woman with her said, "I could use a cup of hot cocoa."

"Of course, Sally. Run along and thank you for your company."

As Sally skated away Gideon offered Rebecca his arm. "Ready?"

"When you are."

He pushed off and wobbled badly. She grasped his arm tightly to hold him up. "Careful."

He was glad she couldn't see embarrassment written all over his face. "Sorry. Guess I'm out of practice."

"It will come back to you," she assured him.

Gideon pushed off again and stayed upright. After a few moments they fell into an easy rhythm as they glided side by side.

They passed several older couples including her grandfather and his wife taking a slow, stately journey around the perimeter. Three boys shot past them racing each other and weaving in and out of their fellow skaters with juvenile recklessness.

Rebecca let go of Gideon and extended her arms out from her sides. "I love skating. It almost feels like flying."

Grasping her fingers lightly, he said, "Almost."

She lowered her arms. "Do you miss it terribly?"

"Yes."

She didn't say anything else. They continued to glide over the ice in a comfortable silence. He was deeply aware of the woman by his side. The need to hold her in his arms and kiss her was overwhelming. The need to protect her and make her his own grew stronger every day. This wasn't the kind of love he'd known in the past.

Oh, he had loved Rebecca when he was young, but it was a pale thing compared to the emotion she awoke in him now. The intensity of his feelings frightened him. What if she couldn't love him back?

She let go of his hand again, this time to spin in a tight circle. Then, with a spray of ice, she stopped abruptly. She was breathing hard and smiling. She said, "Let me see you do that."

"Okay." He turned around once slowly. "How was that?"

"Your technique needs work."

"Are you blind? That was perfect."

She skated toward him. "Perfectly awful."

He stood still until her outstretched hands touched

his chest. He captured them beneath his own, wishing neither of them were wearing gloves. He wanted to feel her touch on his bare skin. He wanted to cup her face between his hands and kiss her until they were both breathless.

She moved back and he let her. This wasn't the time or the place to reveal the depth of his emotions. He would be patient and wait for her no matter how long it took.

Reaching out with one hand she said, "I believe I'm ready for some hot chocolate now."

"As you wish." He led her across the ice and warned her when she reached the edge. She followed his instructions and found the bench with one hand.

Sitting down, she said, "Goodness, I didn't realize how tired I was."

"Does your chemotherapy make you tired?"

"A little."

"Is your treatment going well? Adam told me you won't be able to have the surgery unless you respond to the drugs they are giving you."

"Dr. White assures me all is going as hoped. I'm afraid to believe that."

He left her and returned a few minutes later with two steaming cups in his hands. He gave her one and sat beside her. Gideon sipped his hot drink but it was Rebecca's nearness that kept the afternoon chill at bay.

The trio of speed skaters went flying past again. A group of the girls on the sidelines began egging them on. Elam's booming voice called for an official race. The pleasure skaters happily moved aside. Start and finish lines were set up and a track outlined by spectators. A dozen boys took their places.

Bishop Zook raised his hand. "Three times around. Go!"

Cheers broke out as families urged on their favorites. With nearly everyone out on the ice, he and Rebecca were alone on the bench.

Rebecca set her empty cup aside. "I remember some wonderful skating parties when we were young. Grace could fly like lightning on the ice. She beat every boy who raced her."

A cloud of unhappiness settled over Rebecca's face. It broke Gideon's heart to see her joy turned to sadness. He took her hand to offer his comfort. "Rebecca, what happened? I know the two of you were very close."

Gideon's touch startled her. She wanted to pull away, but the kindness in his voice held her fast. She could feel the warmth of his touch even through her mittens. As Booker once told her, she was woman enough to sense the bond forming between her and Gideon. She thought she knew where he wanted this relationship to go but everything was happening too fast.

Was she ready to start down the path he offered?

A long time ago she turned aside from the love Gideon offered because of Grace. She lost her sight and her one true love. Was it possible that God would restore both to her? Had she truly been forgiven?

"Rebecca, I can see you are troubled. Sometimes it helps to talk."

His gentle encouragement brought tears to her eyes. "Grace has been on my mind a lot lately. Do you remember the time she and I went to a hoedown with you?"

"It was the only time you came to one of those wild parties."

"I wish I hadn't gone even that once."

"You were with me most of that night. Did something happen to you?"

"Not to me. To Grace. She said you thought I was hopelessly uncool, a scaredy cat. That's why I went. I wanted to impress you with how modern I could be. Maybe I wanted to impress my sister a little, too."

"I never thought you were uncool. I thought you were everything an Amish woman should be."

"You were wrong."

"I know it was the first hoedown you both went to, but I saw Grace plenty of times after that. Your sister liked to party."

"Do you remember her boyfriend?"

"Not really. I remember that my brother wanted to court her but she wasn't interested in him."

"That was because she had started going out with an English boy. He was trouble, but she couldn't see it."

"What kind of trouble?"

"Drugs. Grace became an addict."

"I'm sorry. I didn't know."

"No one knew for a long time, but I suspected something was wrong after that night."

"It is truly sad that the plague of drugs has reached into our Amish communities. Has your sister sought help for her addiction?"

"Several times that I know of, but each time she has fallen back into the pit. It has such a powerful hold on her mind."

"Is that why your parents no longer speak of her?"

"They poured their hearts and their money into trying to help her. She used their love to feed her habit for years, begging for money, stealing things from our home to sell for drugs. When she was arrested for selling drugs to other Amish girls Bishop Stoltzfus told my parents that she was lost to them. He forbade us to have any contact with her. If we did, we would be placed under the ban, too. It was a terrible time for them. I could have prevented it all."

"You can't blame yourself for her choices."

"You don't understand. The night of the party, I

saw her boyfriend buying drugs. I overheard him telling his friends that he and Grace were going to get high, but I didn't warn her. She knew I didn't like him. I didn't think she would believe me, but I should have told her. I should have made her listen me."

"Rebecca, taking drugs was still her decision."

"No, it wasn't. She told me later that he put them in her drink. She didn't know what she was taking. It wasn't just at that party although that was the start. She sneaked out to see him almost every night that summer. She was hooked on the drugs before she knew what was happening to her."

"Rebecca, you don't know that Grace would have listened to you even if you had warned her."

"She blames me. She told me so. I was older. It was my responsibility to watch out for her. I turned a blind eye to her when she was in danger and God punished me because of that. How right she was."

"And you think that is why you lost your sight?"

"It was a just punishment. Grace lost her soul because of me. I don't want to go into surgery until I know for certain if she has forgiven me."

He was silent for a long moment. Rebecca could hear the cheers of the crowd spike then die down. Someone had won. Others had lost.

Gideon asked, "Do you know where she lives? Can you reach out to her?"

He didn't tell her she was being foolish. She could

have kissed him for that. His understanding gave her the courage to make her next request. If he refused, she didn't know where else to turn. She squeezed his hand. "I don't know where she is. Will you help me find her?"

Chapter Eleven

Gideon hadn't expected this. Rebecca was asking him to help her find her runaway sister, a sister she was forbidden to contact. What if her family or Bishop Stoltzfus found out about it?

The bishop would jump at the chance to excommunicate Gideon again. He had accepted Gideon's confession, but he made it clear he wouldn't tolerate any transgressions against the *Ordnung*. His attitude was the reason Gideon's family had arranged for him to stay with Adam. While Gideon had been attending church services in Hope Springs, he wasn't an official member of Bishop Zook's congregation. He belonged to Bishop Stoltzfus's church, as did Rebecca's parents.

Gideon knew his actions could have serious repercussions. If it were discovered that he helped Rebecca against the bishop's express wishes, he would forfeit his ability to see his family. It was a lot to risk after all he'd given up to return to the fold.

He looked down at the woman holding his hand. That she trusted him enough to ask such a favor was heady knowledge. He was only beginning to understand the extent of the suffering she endured in silence during the years he was gone. He had sought her forgiveness to make a fresh start in his life. How could he deny her the same blessing?

Many of the skaters were leaving the ice and coming their way. Rebecca tugged her hand from his. He let go reluctantly. Part of the reason he'd given up his career and everything he'd worked for was simply for the right to reenter her life. How could he refuse her request?

He asked, "What if you can't find her before your surgery date? It's only ten days away."

"I will go to New York because so many people have worked to make it possible. I am not ungrateful, but I know the chances of recovering my vision are slim."

"Slim because the surgery is difficult, or because you feel you don't deserve to see?"

"You are as astute as an English fellow I met recently. Or perhaps my face is easier to read than I think."

"Rebecca, forgiveness begins in our own hearts."

"I know that."

"So you profess, but you have not forgiven yourself for the mistakes of your past. Your guilt is a useless burden."

She turned her face away from him. "I expected you to understand. You sought the forgiveness of your family, my forgiveness. How is what I seek any different?"

He pressed his lips into a tight line. She was right about that. He carried his own share of guilt. "I do understand. I will see what I can find out."

Her head came up. "You will?"

"Where was she the last you knew?"

"Millersburg."

"I'll make a few calls. If she was arrested, the sheriff should have a last known address for her. I can use the computer at the public library to search for her online."

"Thank you, Gideon. You know the English ways and how they live. If anyone can find her, I'm sure it is you. Each day I find new reasons to be grateful God has returned you to us."

Daniel Hershberger walked up to them. "Rebecca, would you take a turn around the pond with me?"

She nodded. "Of course."

Gideon watched her skate away with Daniel. Under his breath Gideon said, "It's not your gratitude that I want, Rebecca. It's your love."

Three days after the skating party, Vera dropped Rebecca in front of the doctor's office for her treatment. As Rebecca unfolded her cane, she said, "Don't wait on me today. I have some errands I'd like to run and then I'm meeting a friend for supper so I will be late coming home."

"A date for supper? Can I hope this friend is Daniel Hershberger?"

Rebecca forced herself to smile, but she couldn't lie. "I would rather not say."

Gideon had stopped by their farm that morning. Luckily, Vera had been outside feeding the chickens and gathering eggs. Gideon had an address and he was willing to go with her today.

"Oh, a secret, is it?" Vera chuckled. "That is the way courtships should be. I will not wait up." With a slap of the reins, she set her buggy in motion.

Inside the clinic building, Rebecca waited her turn to see the doctor. When his nurse, Amber, called Rebecca's name, Rebecca followed her to the exam room. When the door was closed behind them, Rebecca said, "I have heard there is a new woman in town that offers rides to the Amish. I think her name is Miriam Kauffman?"

"Yes, I met her at church last Sunday. She was raised Amish but didn't join the Amish faith and moved away. She came back to help her mother when her father became ill. He passed away not long ago."

"Would you call her and see if she is free today? I have a trip I'd like to make."

"Of course. I'll have our receptionist give her a call. Mrs. Nolan keeps a list of everyone who can help with transportation. Do you want me to check if Samson Carter is free, too?"

"Nee." Samson was a gossip. Rebecca didn't want news of her visit getting back to her family.

After her lab tests and the infusion of her chemo, Rebecca returned to the waiting room. Wilma Nolan, the doctor's elderly receptionist, said, "I called Miss Kauffman. She is free today and can provide you with taxi services. Shall I call her back and tell her you're ready to go?"

"That will be fine. *Danki.*"

"Just have a seat, and I'll let you know when she arrives."

Rebecca sat and waited with growing dread. Was this the right thing to do? Would Miriam be discreet, or would she spread gossip about who and where she drove folks?

Rebecca didn't have long to fret. A few minutes later, she heard the door to the clinic open. A woman's voice asked quietly, "Are you Rebecca Beachy?"

Rebecca rose to her feet. "I am."

"Where can I take you?"

Unaware of who might be listening, Rebecca decided against giving out the address. Instead, she said, "I have directions in my purse. I'll find them for you when we are in the car."

"Okay, fine. How do we do this?"

Rebecca held out her hand. "If I take your arm, it's easy for me to follow you."

Outside, Miriam asked, "Do you want to sit in the front seat or the back?"

"The back. Someone will be joining me." Once she was seated, Rebecca waited until Miriam got in on the driver's side. When she heard the door close, she held out a slip of paper. "We need to pick up another passenger at the Wadler Inn, then I'd like you to take us to this address."

"375 North Broadway in New Philadelphia, is that right?"

"Ja." If Grace lived there, Rebecca wasn't sure what she would say to her sister. No, she knew what she would say. What she was afraid of was her sister's answer. What if Grace couldn't forgive? What then?

The drive to the Wadler Inn took only a few minutes. When the car stopped, the door beside Rebecca opened and she heard Gideon get in.

Miriam asked, "Are we waiting on anyone else?"

"No," Gideon answered.

"Okay, then, we're off."

The first few miles of the trip were spent in silence. Rebecca was too nervous to engage in chitchat. Finally, it was Gideon who spoke. "I understand you are ex-Amish, Miss Kauffman?"

"I chose not to be baptized. It wasn't the life for

me. I grew up near Millersburg. My family was Swartzentruber Amish."

The Swartzentruber Amish were a strict Old Order sect. They lived austere lives even by Amish standards. They had no indoor plumbing. They didn't allow cushions on their furniture. Nor did they allow lights or the reflective orange triangles on their buggies that warned they were slow-moving vehicles in spite of the dangers. Their teenagers did not enjoy a rumspringa, but were expected to join the faith without question.

Gideon said, "I've heard Swartzentruber young people who don't choose baptism are shunned by their families."

"They are. My family had a falling-out with the bishop in their church district after I left. They moved to Hope Springs a few years ago and joined a more liberal church. When my father became ill, my mother asked me to return."

"Not all bishops are created equal. I can vouch for that." Gideon's voice held a hint of bitterness.

Rebecca thought of all he had gone through to make the transition back the Amish life and still the bishop of his former congregation did not welcome him.

Gideon leaned close to Rebecca. "You look nervous."

"I shouldn't be. I'm only going to visit my sister. Are you sure we will find her in New Philadelphia?"

"This is the only address the sheriff had for her. It's more than a year old. She might not be there, but at least she hasn't been in trouble with the law in the last thirteen months."

"Gideon, I appreciate your help with this. I would not have known where to start."

"I guess my time in the outside world wasn't a complete waste. I was able to use the computer at the public library. I'm glad I could help, Rebecca. I'm glad you asked me."

His last words, spoken so softly against her ear, sent shivers down her spine and filled her with excitement. If she turned her face a little their lips would meet. He wanted to kiss her. She knew it. What surprised her was how much she wanted to be kissed by him.

She faced straight ahead. After a moment, he moved away but she wasn't able to relax. The ride seemed to take forever. Gideon tried to put her at ease by relating things he saw along the roadside. Any other time, she would have appreciated his kindness. Today, she was too keyed up.

At long last, Miriam said, "This is New Philadelphia."

Rebecca sat up straight. "Is it a big city? How will we find her address?"

"GPS," Miriam and Gideon said at the same time. Then they both laughed.

Rebecca had no idea what they were talking about

or why it was funny. Gideon had much more in common with their English driver than she did.

He said, "This is a nice midsize. How's the gas mileage?"

"Thirty-two highway. Not bad."

"That's better than my Audi SS got."

"You drove an SS? I've always wanted one. Do they handle as well as people say?"

"Better. It's a sweet machine. Zero to sixty in nothing flat. I was sorry to sell it."

"I can imagine. Still, it would have looked funny being pulled by a horse, even in Amish country."

"I might have gotten by with it. It was black." He was joking, but Rebecca sensed how much he missed the vehicle he once owned. How could he be content with a horse and buggy after driving fast cars and flying planes?

Miriam made several turns and finally came to a stop. She said, "I believe this is it."

Rebecca reached for Gideon's hand and squeezed his fingers tightly. "What do you see? What kind of house is it?"

"It's a nice neighborhood. The house is an older home with a porch that wraps around it on two sides. It's two stories tall and painted blue with white trim. There are white shutters on the windows. And…"

"And what?" she insisted.

"It doesn't look like the kind of place a drug addict would hang out."

"That is *goot,* isn't it?"

"Maybe. Or maybe we have the wrong address. I guess there is only one way to find out." He pushed open the car door.

Rebecca wanted to follow him but her body wouldn't move.

Please Lord, give me the courage I need.

Gideon said, "You didn't come this far to sit in a car."

"*Nee.* I did not." Forcing her trembling muscles to move, Rebecca scooted out of the car and stood.

"I will be right beside you," he said quietly. Taking her hand, he tucked it in the crook of his elbow and started forward. Rebecca had no choice but to follow him.

He said, "We're at the front steps. There are five of them. There is a handrail on your left side."

Grasping the rail, she walked up the steps. The boards of the porch creaked as Gideon led her across them. "We are at the front door. Do you want me to ring the bell?"

Her body was shaking, but she managed to nod. "I did not come all this way just to stand on the porch."

"That's my girl."

She wasn't his girl, but she liked the sound of that.

Gideon rang the bell. Inside the house, the chime played a brief tune.

When the door opened, Rebecca braced herself. Only it wasn't her sister's voice she heard. A man asked, "Can I help you?"

Rebecca spoke up. "We are looking for Grace Beachy. Does she live here?"

"Beachy was my wife's maiden name. May I ask who you are?"

"I am her sister."

"Really? My wife never mentioned she had a sister. Are you sure you have the right house?" His voice grew suspicious.

Grace was married. Perhaps she had found happiness far from her past. Rebecca prayed it was so.

"Who is it, dear?" It was Grace's voice. Rebecca heard footsteps approaching and then a sudden, harsh intake of breath.

She said, "Hello, Grace."

"Rebecca? Is it really you?"

"*Ja.* I'm so glad I found you."

"Why did you come here? Why?" There was such pain in her sister's voice. She wanted to reach out and gather Grace into her arms.

Grace's husband said, "Honey, what's going on?"

"Clearly, a blast from my past. It's all right, Randy. I'll explain everything later."

He lowered his voice, but confusion colored his tone. "You told me your family was dead."

"I'm dead to them. They are dead to me."

Gideon spoke up. "We'll only take a few minutes of your time. May we come in?"

Rebecca said, "This is my friend Gideon Troyer."

"It's been a long time, Grace. You may not remember me."

"You're Levi Troyer's older brother."

"That's right."

"I never thought you'd return to the Plain folk."

Grace sounded so bitter. Rebecca saw her chances of making amends with her sister slipping away.

"Life has a way of changing what we see as important. May we come in?" Gideon asked again.

"I guess." The door creaked slightly as Grace opened it wider.

Rebecca was grateful for Gideon's solid presence beside her as she entered the house. They took a seat on a sofa. The room simmered with tension. Rebecca prayed for wisdom. She wanted her sister's forgiveness. She needed it.

Grace's husband asked, "Can I get you anything? Something to drink?"

Rebecca shook her head. "No, *danki*...thank you."

Grace said, "Randy, why don't you take Mr. Troyer outside and show him your greenhouse? I'd like to speak to Rebecca alone."

"Are you sure, hon?"

"Yes."

After the two men left the room, Grace said,

"Randy has ten green thumbs. He would have made a good farmer. Fortunately for me, he's a banker."

Rebecca took a deep breath. "The reason I have come is to beg your forgiveness, sister, for the way I failed you when we were young."

"You're asking for my forgiveness? Wow. That's not the way I thought this conversation would go if it ever happened."

Rebecca sensed that she was entering an emotional quagmire. One false step and all would be lost. "I, too, have thought about this day. Many times. I have missed you."

"You miss a naive sixteen-year-old Amish girl. I haven't been that person in a long time."

"I miss my sister."

"But not enough to look for me in last eight years."

"You know the reason I could not seek you out."

"Sure. So what has changed? Are Mom and Dad okay?"

Rebecca realized the tension in her sister's voice wasn't anger. It was fear. She thought Rebecca had come to deliver bad news. "*Mamm* and *Daed* are the same as always. She complains that he spends too much time gossiping with neighbors. He complains that she enjoys bossing him around."

With a nervous laugh, Grace said, "She does enjoy bossing him around."

"Very much so. Grace, how did you think this conversation would go?"

"I never really thought it would happen. I was always afraid I'd run into someone from the family on the street or in the new superstore that opened two years ago. In my mind, I could see the stunned looks and then the inevitable question. Have I repented my evil ways? It never occurred to me that you would seek me out. Not once did I think you would be here begging *my* forgiveness."

"I am begging it now. As you told me so long ago, I failed to protect you when you needed your big sister the most."

"I said that?"

"You did, and you were right. The night we went to the hoedown together I saw your boyfriend buying drugs. I tried to find you to tell you his intentions, but I didn't find you until it was too late."

"Too late for what?"

"He'd already put the drugs in your drink. My failure led to your downfall. Months later you told me what happened. If I had warned you…you never would have become addicted to that terrible stuff. I could have saved you."

"What else did I say?"

"That God had punished me by taking away my sight. I knew you were right."

"That's cold. Was I high when I said it?"

Puzzled, Rebecca frowned. "We were at home. Don't you remember the day I found the drugs you'd hidden in your room?"

"I can't have hidden them very well if a half-blind woman found them. No, Rebecca, I don't remember saying those things, but I'm sure I did."

It had been the most painful day of Rebecca's life. It was the day she learned she would soon be completely blind and there was nothing that could be done for her.

Depressed and suffering in a world growing darker by the day, she cried out asking God why? Grace gave her the answer and she accepted it. That evening she refused Gideon's offer of marriage and shut away all her hopes for the future.

She shook her head as she tried to comprehend what Grace was telling her. "How could you forget saying such a thing to me?"

"I was an addict. I would say or do anything to gain more dope or protect my stash. The night of the hoedown wasn't my first experience with drugs. I sent…wow…I can't even remember his name. I sent him to buy the drugs. I'd been using for months before that."

"What?" Rebecca couldn't believe what she was hearing.

"I started using marijuana when I was fifteen. By the time that hoedown rolled around I had graduated to meth."

"You lied? You lied to me? Why? Why make me believe I was to blame?"

"Because I was an addict. Don't you get it? Addicts don't take responsibility for their actions. They lie, they cheat, they steal, they manipulate and they blame everyone but themselves. It's easier than facing the truth."

Rebecca leaned back into the sofa. It had all been a lie, but Grace's words had changed everything. Because of her, Rebecca told Gideon she couldn't marry him, believing she didn't deserve happiness with him when Grace had suffered so much because of her. She believed God had taken her sight as a way to punish her.

How poor was her faith to believe such a thing of her Father in heaven?

Rebecca jumped when Grace touched her hands. "I'm sorry I lied to you, Rebecca. I'm sorry for the way I treated our parents and for the pain I caused more people than you will ever know. I've been clean for three years now. Although I don't deserve it, I ask your forgiveness."

"I forgive you." Rebecca muttered the words even as she was reeling with grief. She'd lost so much.

"Randy knows I was an addict. He knows I have a record. He has been my second greatest supporter. God has been my first. It seems odd to say an Amish girl found God in rehab, but that is exactly what happened. Faith is a tricky thing. You can be raised with it all around you, but if you don't open your heart to God, you will never truly know Him."

"I'm happy for you, Grace." Rebecca rose to her

feet. She heard the sound of a door open and the murmur of male voices.

"Tell the family that I did manage to turn my life around. Do you think there is any chance that Mom and Dad would come for a visit?"

The quiver in Grace's voice touched Rebecca deeply. She had hoped to find forgiveness here. Instead, she was the one who needed to forgive. She had already uttered the words, but in this moment, she knew the truth of them in her soul.

"I will do my best to convince them." Rebecca held open her arms and the baby sister she prayed would forgive her rushed into them.

Chapter Twelve

Gideon stopped in the doorway to Grace's living room and smiled at the sight of Rebecca with Grace in her arms. The two women looked so much alike that they could have been twins. One English, one Amish.

From the expression on their faces, he decided that at least one of his prayers had been answered. Rebecca had gained the forgiveness she sought.

Grace's husband said to him, "Maybe we should go back to the greenhouse."

Grace pulled away from Rebecca and wiped the tears from her cheeks. "Don't be silly. We were just saying goodbye."

Rebecca managed to smile. "I will write and share all the family news with you."

Grace nodded. "That will be a good start. It's going to take me a while to explain to Randy how many in-laws he actually has."

"I can't promise he will ever get to meet them," Rebecca said quietly.

Grace took her hand. "I know, but it means the world to me that you came."

"I will come again when I can stay longer. I must get back now."

Grace extended her hand to Gideon. "Thank you for bringing her here."

"You're welcome. Did she tell you about her surgery?"

Grace glanced from his face to Rebecca's. "No. What surgery?"

"There is a doctor in New York who thinks she can restore Rebecca's sight."

"There's no guarantee," Rebecca added quickly.

Grace cupped Rebecca's face in her hands. "Nothing is beyond His powers. I will pray for your healing."

The sisters embraced once more and then Gideon led Rebecca out to the car where Miriam sat reading a book. She closed it when she saw them and got out to open the door.

"Did you have a nice visit?"

"*Ja,* it was *goot,*" was all Rebecca said.

She was quiet all the way back to Hope Springs. He had little to do but watch the snow-covered countryside slide past. He wanted to press her about her conversation with her sister but he didn't want to do it in front of Miriam.

At the inn, Rebecca got out with him. When the car pulled away, she said, "My thanks for arranging this, Gideon."

"Let me get my horse and buggy, and I'll drop you off on my way home. You can wait inside the inn for me."

She raised her face to the cold evening air. "I don't feel like going inside. Where do you keep your horse?"

"Naomi Wadler lives behind the inn. She lets me keep Homer in her little stable when I'm working in town. She says her mare likes the company."

"What does the sky look like tonight, Gideon?"

He took her hand and placed it in the crook of his arm. "The sun is going down. There are high clouds above us."

They began walking. "What kind of clouds?" she asked.

"Cirrus clouds." She looked puzzled so he said, "Mares' tails."

"I remember them. They're curly wisps high in the air. They mean the weather is going to change in a day or so. Have you flown through them?"

"Cirrus clouds normally form above twenty thousand feet. That's higher than my type of plane would typically fly." He wasn't sure what to make of the mood she was in. She seemed pensive. Had he been mistaken about her visit with Grace?

"When I hear the sound of a plane engine in the

sky I wonder where they are going in such a hurry. Where did you fly to?"

"Many places. I often took passengers on sightseeing flights over the Great Lakes. I carried supplies up to remote areas in Canada or fishermen on a wilderness holiday. I took fresh fruit to markets in the Midwest. I took a grandmother to see her new grandson on Drummond Island. Every day was different."

"It must have been exciting."

"That it was."

"There isn't much excitement in Hope Springs when an ice-skating party is the biggest thing to happen all week."

"It can get quiet here. I'm still not used to the businesses closing up at five. No all-night grocery stores, no fast-food places open at one in the morning, no traffic on the roads. I'd give almost anything for a pizza place that stays open until midnight."

When she didn't speak, he wondered what she was thinking. Finally, she asked, "Are the clouds tinted red and gold by the sunset?"

"The sun is below the horizon so they're barely pink now. It won't be long before it's full dark."

"Then everyone will see what I see." She fell silent. He didn't know what to say.

They reached the stable a few minutes later. Sliding open the door, Gideon was greeted by a whinny from Homer. Rebecca said, "He sounds happy to see you."

"Homer thinks he's going to get a treat." A second whinny followed from Naomi's little mare.

Rebecca smiled. "She is hoping for one, too. If Homer has to go out on a cold night, he should have a treat. Where do you keep them?"

"Hold out your hands." She did, and he poured a cup of alfalfa nuggets into her palms from a pail hanging on a hook. He led her forward until she was standing at the stall door. Homer stretched his neck out and began to nibble them up.

When her hands were empty, she dusted them together. Reaching out, she located Homer's face and scratched him under his chin. "What color is he?"

"He's a dark dapple gray. His sire was a Percheron. He's not a fast horse, but he gets the job done."

"I imagine he's pretty."

"Not so much. He's got a Roman nose and sloping shoulders."

"You have to look past his physical defects. On the inside he is pretty."

"So are you. Inside and out." Gideon held his breath waiting for her reply. He wanted her to know he still cared for her, but he wasn't sure she was ready to hear that.

"That is kind of you to say." It was too dark in the barn to tell if she was blushing, but he suspected she was. She moved down the aisle to where Naomi's mare stood with her head over the stall door watching the activity.

Gideon harnessed Homer and led him outside. It took him a few minutes to hitch up. When he went back inside the barn, he saw Rebecca sitting on the floor. She was crying. He rushed forward. "What's wrong?"

"Nothing. I'm being foolish, that's all." She drew her knees up to her chin and wrapped her arms around them.

He sat beside her on the dirt floor. "It isn't foolish to cry. You've had an emotional day."

"It wasn't at all what I expected."

"Are you sorry you went?"

"*Nee,* I'm not, but I'm sorry for many other things."

"Like what?"

She drew a deep breath. "It doesn't matter. I can't put spilled milk back in the glass. Forgive my bout of self-pity. We should be getting home. I don't want Vera to start worrying."

Reluctantly, Gideon rose and helped her to her feet. As he held her hand a moment longer, he fought the urge to wrap his arms around her and draw her close. He needed to hold her as much as he needed his next breath.

Rebecca wanted nothing more than to throw herself into Gideon's embrace and erase the years they had wasted. He had offered his friendship. Did she have the right to ask for more after sending him away all those years ago?

Would he welcome her advances or would he rebuff her? Or would he pity her, a blind old maid looking for love where there was none.

She wasn't brave enough to find out. If only she could read the truth in his eyes.

After her surgery, God willing, she might be able to see for herself. If the surgery healed her. If Gideon was still here when she came home.

She'd felt how at ease he was with Miriam in the car. It was familiar for him. She'd heard the longing in his voice when he spoke about his car, about flying and the parts of the English world that he missed. Would his faith hold him here against the freedoms he'd known and given up?

Only time would tell. She had to fight this attraction she had for him. She couldn't stand loving and losing him all over again.

Stepping away from him, she withdrew her cane from the pocket of her coat and extended it. "Please take me home. I have one of my headaches coming on."

She found her way to the stable door and to the buggy outside. Gideon helped her in and then went around to the other side. The buggy dipped on its springs as he climbed in. The motion tipped her toward him. Her shoulder came in contact with his.

She didn't move away. If this were the only closeness she could share with him, she would accept that. For now. If the surgery made her whole, things might be different. For the first time, she allowed herself to hope for her own recovery.

Gideon clicked his tongue and set Homer in motion. The plodding clop of his hooves, the jingle of the harness and the drone of the tires on the pavement were the only sounds as they drove out of town.

The following morning, Gideon entered the office at the Wadler Inn to meet with Adam about what service calls were scheduled for the day. Adam's high-quality repair work brought back repeat customers both in and outside of Hope Springs. When he married Emma and became part owner of the inn, he had trouble keeping up with the demands on his time. Gideon was thrilled to work for Adam. It gave him a chance to use the skills he had acquired during his time in the English world. Adam was easygoing and a good boss to work for.

Adam looked up from his desk and the pile of paperwork in front of him. "Good, you're here. Reuben Beachy stopped by looking for you."

Gideon's heart skipped a beat. Had Rebecca's grandfather found out about their visit to Grace? Was he angry that Gideon had helped Rebecca arrange it? Gideon tried to keep his trepidation hidden. "Did he say what he wanted?"

"His used cutting machine has arrived."

Gideon relaxed only slightly. "I'll drop over and see if I can get it running for him."

After leaving the inn, Gideon walked through Hope Springs and down the back alley leading to Reuben's store. A new store stood where only ashes had been a few weeks ago, but the style of the shop was the same. Gideon entered through the back door.

The faint smell of smoke still lingered in the air triggering a rush of memories. Gideon felt the heat of the flames on his face. He felt the smoke burning his lungs. His brain screamed at him to get out.

"*Goot* day, Gideon Troyer." Reuben's jovial voice pulled Gideon out of the darkness. He was in a bright new workroom. There were fewer tack pieces on display, but a new workbench had replaced the old one at the side of the room and new tools hung from their slots.

Gideon nodded to Reuben. "I understand you have some new equipment you'd like me to look at."

"*Ja.* I will show you."

Reuben led the way to a machine in the corner. Gideon set down his toolbox and squatted beside it to examine the motor first. "Have you tried turning it on?"

"What do you think of my new shop, Booker? The place looks much different than the last time you were here."

Gideon looked up and met Reuben's sharp eyes. His hope that the old man wouldn't recognize him died a quick death. "How long have you known?"

"From the first moment I saw you. Rebecca is the only blind one in my family."

Gideon rose to his feet. "I'm sorry for the deception. I felt I had to keep my identity a secret when I came for the auction. I was under the ban, but I wanted to help Rebecca. I thought if she knew who I was she would refuse the money I paid for her quilt."

"I expect she would have done so, but dishonesty, no matter how noble the cause, is still dishonesty, Booker."

Gideon folded his arms. "I wanted to help. I had no intention of staying in Hope Springs, but the weather kept me in town and I maintained my disguise."

"Why?"

"So that I could spend time with Rebecca. We were close once. I wanted to know why she suddenly turned her back on me when I asked her to marry me."

"And did you discover the reason?"

"I discovered that I still cared deeply for Rebecca."

"This is why you came back here?"

"It was more than my feeling for Rebecca that made me return. I saw things when I was Booker that I missed more than I knew. I missed the closeness to God that the Amish have. I missed the sense of family and community. I wanted to become a part of that again."

"And?"

"I didn't realize how empty my life was until I saw Rebecca again. I wanted a chance to win her heart."

"A woman is a poor reason to take up the yoke of our faith."

"I'd like to think Rebecca is the instrument God used to bring me back to my senses and back to our faith. I did not make my confession lightly. I meant every word."

Reuben stroked his beard as he pondered Gideon's words. "Many an Amish lad might have left the faith but for the Amish lass who caught his eye. Myself included. What do you intend to do?"

"Live Amish. I already have a job. I'm renting a house. One day I will build a home of my own. I plan to court Rebecca, and I pray daily that she finds it in her heart to become my wife."

"Have you told her you are the one she calls Booker?"

"No."

Reuben's shaggy eyebrows rose on his forehead. "You have not? Why?"

"Because Booker is gone. All that Booker was ended when I knelt before my father and begged his forgiveness. Rebecca is grateful to the man who paid for her surgery. I don't want her gratitude. I wanted Rebecca to know and love me, Gideon Troyer."

"For such a smart man, you've been pretty stupid."

Gideon swallowed hard. "Are you going to tell her?"

"I will not. That is between the two of you. I understand your motives even if I don't agree with them. You know her surgery may not give her back her sight."

"That makes no difference to the way I feel about her."

"Then I have something to ask of you. Soon, Rebecca and Vera will travel to New York City. Do you know this place?"

"I've been there many times."

"I have read much about the city. I do not think it is a place I want my daughter and my granddaughter to travel alone."

"Are you saying you don't want Rebecca to have the surgery?"

"*Nee,* I'm asking you to travel with them. To see that they make it safely there and back. Will you do this for me?"

"I will."

"Goot."

"How will they travel there?"

"We have not decided. Perhaps by train from Akron, perhaps we will hire a driver for the entire trip."

"The train will take a full day. The drive is nine hours at least. It would be better to fly from Akron."

"Our ways are not about convenience, Booker. Gideon should know this."

"You're right. A day's worth of travel is not a hardship. I will find a driver for Rebecca and Vera."

"*Goot.* Now let us see if we can get this machine running. I have many orders to fill."

Gideon hooked the motor to a car battery and turned the switch to start the propane-powered engine. The machine roared to life. He looked over his shoulder at Reuben leaning over him. "I don't see anything wrong with this."

"*Wunderbaar!* You are a fine mechanic, Gideon Troyer."

Standing, Gideon gathered his unopened tool chest. "And you are a sneaky fellow, Reuben Beachy."

Two days later, Gideon rounded a curve in the road on his way to town. The bright sunshine of the early morning had given way to encroaching clouds pushed by a sharp north wind. As was his habit when he passed Vera's farm, he glanced toward the two-story frame house set back from the road in hopes of spotting Rebecca. The yard and lane were empty. Not that he really expected her to be standing out in the snow.

He slapped the lines against Homer's rump. The gelding picked up the pace and put his head down as he started up the steep hill past Vera's lane. As they reached the top, Gideon passed an Amish woman walking along the highway. To his surprise, it was Rebecca. She was heading toward Hope Springs.

He pulled to a stop and got out. "Would you be needing a ride? I have room."

She stopped. Indecision flitted across her face but the next gust of cold wind settled matters. "*Ja,* a ride would be most welcome. It wasn't this cold when I started out."

Gideon took her arm and guided her to the buggy. "What are you doing walking to town?"

"Vera's arthritis is giving her a great deal of pain today. I can do a lot of things, but I can't drive a horse. So I must walk to town to see Dr. White."

He climbed in beside her and closed the door. It was warmer out of the wind. "Is it the day for your chemo?"

She nodded. "Three days a week I must go and be poked and prodded to make sure the drugs are helping and not hurting me."

"Do the treatments make you sick?"

"Nee." She didn't seem inclined to elaborate.

He set the horse in motion. He'd been hoping to spend time alone with Rebecca ever since he arrived in Hope Springs. Now that he had her to himself, he didn't know what to say. He could see the outskirts of the town ahead. He didn't have much time left. Homer wasn't speedy by any stretch of the imagination, but it wouldn't take him long to cover the last half mile.

Feeling the pressure, Gideon decided it was best to take the bull by the horns. "Your grandfather has asked that I go with you and Vera to New York when you travel there for your surgery."

"Why on earth would Grandfather suggest such a thing?"

"He feels I will have a better understanding of the English city. He thinks my presence will make things easier and safer for the two of you."

"Aren't you worried that going out into the English world will provide a great temptation for you?"

"No." Did she still doubt he would remain Amish? The thought was a sobering one. He wanted her to believe in him.

They rode in silence for the next several minutes. Finally, she asked, "Are you so sure your old life will not call you back?"

"Everything I want…no, everything I need in my life is here. Except for one thing."

He glanced at her from the corner of his eye. He

could see the curiosity simmering in her expression. Finally, she asked, "What one thing are you missing?"

"My *mamm* and my friends tell me it's time I looked about for a wife. What do you think?"

Her brow furrowed. "What do you mean, what do I think? It is none of my business if you wish to take a wife."

The subject made her uncomfortable. That was promising. He pressed harder. "You know the women in this community. I haven't been here for very long. Is it too soon for me to be thinking about finding a mate?"

"How should I know?" She was miffed. It meant she cared.

He said, "Women talk. Have any of the women in our church expressed an interest in me?"

"If you are fishing for a compliment, Gideon Troyer, I must tell you your hook is bare."

"I'm not fishing for compliments. I'm just trying to gauge my chances. I'm not all that handsome. I don't have much to offer. I'm a handyman. I'm renting a home. What do people think about me?"

She shrugged then said, "I heard Sally thinks you're handsome. If I remember right, you were a nice-looking fellow."

"*Danki.* Which Sally?"

"Sally Yoder."

"What? She can't be older than seventeen."

"She is nineteen. Old enough to be courting."

"I am not robbing the cradle. I need someone closer to my own age."

"Well, there is Sarah."

He pretended to consider her. "Sarah. Hmm. Has she ever mentioned me?"

"Not within my hearing."

"I'm afraid a widow would always be comparing me to her dead husband. I don't think I would like that. Who else would you suggest?"

She folded her arms. "There is the schoolteacher, Leah Belier. She is in her early twenties."

"No. She's too smart."

"Too smart for you?"

"Too smart to fall for a fellow like me."

"Very true. It would be a foolish woman who set her heart on the likes of you."

"You liked me once," he reminded her to gauge her reaction.

Her chin came up a notch. "I outgrew it. What about Susan Lapp?"

"I am not so desperate as to ask out Susan Lapp."

"'A plump wife and the big barn never did any man harm.'" She recited the old adage with a smirk.

"She's also at least fifteen years older than I am and she likes garlic. I don't think you are taking this seriously."

Crossing her arms, Rebecca blew out a sharp breath. "Very well. What about Helen Bender?"

"Too old."

"Mary Beth Zook?"

"The Bishop's daughter? Would you want Ester Zook as your mother-in-law?"

"You have a point."

She went through a half dozen more suggestions. He found an objection to each and every one and enjoyed watching the play of emotions across her face. She did care for him.

When they reached the medical clinic, Gideon turned the horse into the parking lot in front of the building. He said, "We're here."

He couldn't wait any longer. He had to know if he stood any sort of chance with her. He took her hand in his.

Flustered, she said, "I'm sorry I could not think of a wife to suit you. I fear I have listed everyone in Hope Springs who is single."

He leaned closer, keeping hold of her hand. "Not everyone, Rebecca. You left out the one I have wanted to court all along."

Her fingers twitched nervously in his grasp. "And who might that be?"

He leaned forward and whispered in her ear. "You."

Chapter Thirteen

"What did you say?" Rebecca held her breath. Had she heard Gideon correctly?

"I want to court you, Rebecca Beachy."

"Is this some kind of joke?" she demanded. She could pretend to play along with his wish list of brides, but hearing her heart's most secret wish tossed into the game wasn't funny.

"No. Why would you think that?"

"I'm blind, Gideon. I'm not stupid. I can't be a wife to you or anyone else."

"Why? Because you can't see? Blind people can do almost anything a sighted person can do, just in a different way. You told me that. It takes a heart to love someone, not a pair of eyes."

She turned her face away from him. "Don't do this to me. I sent you away, and you have a right to be angry, but don't punish me for something I did ten years ago."

He cupped his fingers beneath her chin and lifted her face. If only she could read what was in his eyes.

"Rebecca, I'm not trying to punish you. In my own awkward way, I'm trying to tell you that my feelings for you have grown into something deep and wonderful. I love you, Rebecca."

"You don't mean that. You feel sorry for me, that's all."

"Darling, I pray you may one day see the love I have for you written on my face. If it is God's will that you never look upon me, then I will whisper my love to you every day and every night so that you never doubt it."

Slowly, her disbelief was pushed aside by the sincerity in his voice. *Please, Lord, don't let this be a joke at my expense.*

"Gideon, we've only known each other these few short weeks. The feelings we had for each other as children no longer count. We aren't the same people we were back then. Do you expect me to believe this brief time has been long enough for you to grow to love me? I'm not sure it can be."

He sighed heavily. "You would have to be sensible. My timing isn't great. I know that. You have a lot on your mind. I understand this must feel rushed to you. Only, say you will think about what I have said. Trust me when I say I have loved you for a long time. I don't think I ever stopped loving you."

"But you went away. You left without a word."

"Yes, I did. I was a fool. No amount of anger or blame is going to bring back those lost years."

"I shouldn't have brought that up. I'm not angry with you anymore."

"If you can forgive me, you must forgive yourself, too."

She had the chance now to erase the pain she had caused. If she was brave enough to take it. "I will think on all you have said."

She'd spent a decade believing she didn't deserve to be loved. To hear Gideon say that he still loved her was almost more than she could bear. She wasn't ready to share her feelings with him. She wasn't certain how she felt. Her emotions were all jumbled.

"What are your plans, Gideon?"

"To stay."

"Here in Hope Springs?"

"Yes. This is my home now."

It was the right answer, the one she wanted to hear.

He asked, "Would you like me to wait and take you home after you're finished with the doctor?"

"*Nee,* I will enjoy the walk back. It will give me time to think."

"Are you sure? I don't mind waiting."

"I am not a child that must be guarded. You have work you must do. Do not let me keep you from it."

"Spoken like the sensible woman you are. Very well. May I stop by to see you tomorrow evening?"

She smiled. "I would like that."

Rebecca left his buggy and entered the medical clinic with her mind in a whirl. What should she do? What answer should she give him? Her sensible side said wait and see if Gideon could live true to their faith. Her heart cried out to grasp this chance at happiness before it was too late.

When it was her turn to see the doctor, she sat through the battery of tests with barely a thought for them. Finally, Dr. White entered the room and pulled his chair up beside her. "I've just spoken with Dr. Eriksson. We both feel the inflammation in your eyes has improved enough to go ahead with the surgery."

"I thought it would be several more weeks yet."

"Happily, you've responded to this treatment much better than we cxpected."

"How soon does she wish to do the surgery?" Rebecca could barely breathe.

"The day after tomorrow. You're to check into the hospital at seven in the morning. The surgery will take place at ten. If all goes well, you'll find out twenty-four hours later if the surgery was a success."

"I can't believe it's going to happen." She would be home before Christmas. The thought of seeing her family's faces after so many years brought tears to her eyes.

Please, God, let it be possible.

Dr. White said, "Rebecca, I caution you not to get your hopes up. It's possible you won't recover your sight."

"I understand. I have faith, Dr. White. Faith that this surgery and the outcome is God's will."

He laid his hand over hers. "Everyone here will be praying for you."

A whirlwind of packing and preparations followed that afternoon as Emma and Sarah came to help Rebecca and Vera get ready for their trip. With each article of clothing Rebecca put in her suitcase the situation became more real. She was going to New York. If all went well, she would be able to see again. Her hands started shaking at the thought.

Please, please, please, Lord, let me see.

After a sleepless night, Rebecca came down to the kitchen the following morning. Vera was already up ahead of her. She said, "Do I hear a buggy?"

"I don't hear anything."

Vera opened the front door. "Well, bless my soul."

"What is it?" Rebecca moved to stand beside her aunt.

"There are a dozen buggies in the yard and more coming."

Overwhelmed, the two women greeted the people who came to wish them Godspeed and offer prayers for their safe return. By the time Samson Carter pulled his van into the yard at eight o'clock, most of Rebecca's church was waiting to see her off.

On the steps of the house, Bishop Zook pronounced a blessing over Rebecca as her grandfather and her aunt stood beside her gripping her hands. Her heart expanded with love for the gift of her family and friends and she gave thanks for all the people who loved her.

Getting into the van, she found Gideon already seated inside. He asked, "Are you ready for this?"

"I'm not sure."

"Too late now. I've already paid for the van and booked the motel rooms. We're off to the Big Apple."

"I thought we were going to New York," Vera said as she climbed in the front seat beside Samson.

Samson and Gideon chuckled. "So we are," Samson declared.

The first half hour was exciting, but before long the car trip became exhausting for Rebecca. She soon had a headache and a queasy stomach brought on by the motion of the car. At their first stop, a roadside diner in eastern Ohio, Gideon ordered peppermint tea for her and an ice pack which he placed on the back of her neck. It helped, but she knew she was in for a rough day.

Gideon tried to distract her by painting word pictures of the countryside they traveled through. It was easy to imagine the rolling hills, the frozen lakes and rivers and the towns they passed as they traveled east. The occasional snore she heard from her aunt made her envious.

Sometime in the afternoon, she must have dozed off because she awoke with a start to find her head resting on Gideon's shoulder. She started to sit up, but he held her still. "You're fine where you are."

If only he knew how much she wanted to stay exactly where she was.

He asked, "How's the headache?"

"Some better."

"Do you get them often?"

"Once or twice a month. Sometimes they're just headaches, sometime they get very bad. Dr. White calls them migraine headaches. They started after I went blind."

"Are you worried about this surgery?"

"I try not to be, but I can't help it. My faith is not always strong enough."

"You don't have to be strong. You have friends who will be strong for you."

"Friends like you?"

"I'm honored you count me a friend. I will always be that, no matter what decision you make about us."

She didn't want to think about their relationship. She only wanted to stay where she was at the moment. Safe in his arms, her head resting against his chest, listening to his heartbeat. She could hear the strong steady sound beneath her ear. It soothed her fears and gave her strength.

She said, "Tell me what you see outside the windows."

"It's dark now. We're passing a small town. I see Christmas lights outlining the rooftops. Some are twinkling like the stars in the sky, some burn a steady red or blue. There are plastic reindeer in the front yard of the house we just passed. The one beside it has two blow-up plastic snowmen in their yard. I see a tall toy soldier down the block."

"The English chose a funny way to celebrate the birth of our savior. He came among us in a lowly stable. There were no lights or toys to announce his coming."

"Many English know the true meaning of Christmas. We can only pray those who don't will find it in their hearts to believe."

"How did you celebrate the day when you lived out in the world?"

"Sometimes I went to church with the woman who worked for me. Usually, I spent it alone. Christmas was a sad time for me after I left home. I missed my family. I missed going to the schoolhouse to watch the children give their program. Remember the year you and I had a poem to recite together?"

"I do. I messed up my lines and I cried. You were so kind to me later."

"I had to make up for cutting the ties off your *kapp* somehow."

She chuckled at the memory. "What will you do this year?"

"My parents and most of my family are coming to spend it with me. I'm not sure where I'll put everyone in my house, but I sure will enjoy my mother's cooking. I told her I'd like a big pan of her peach cobbler and pot roast with biscuits. She makes the best biscuits."

"You say that, but you haven't had one of mine."

"Are you a good cook?"

"I have a certain talent with biscuits."

"Are they light?"

"So light you have to hold a pot over the oven door to catch them when they float out."

"But are they flaky?"

"So flaky that they have been mistaken for the pages of a book."

"I *lieb* flaky biscuits with butter and honey. How is your shoo-fly pie?"

"Passable."

"Eli Imhoff says I should marry a good cook because good looks fade but good cooking doesn't."

Rebecca giggled. "I don't doubt that Nettie keeps him well fed."

"What will you do for Christmas?"

"Vera and I will be at home for Christmas Day with my grandfather and his wife. We plan to travel to my parents' home for old Christmas. After that, we will go to see my brother in Indiana."

"Perhaps all of you could come and spend Christmas Day with my family," he suggested.

"I would like that. I know my grandfather would, too. We haven't spoken to your parents in many years."

"I know my mother will be delighted to visit with you, but be prepared."

"For what?"

"Many hints and suggestions about me. She wishes to see me married."

"Is that why you're on the lookout for a wife?"

"I'm not on the lookout for a wife. I've found the woman I want. I'm content to wait and see if she wants me."

"For how long?"

"As long as it takes her to make up her mind. Enough about that. Try and go back to sleep." He settled lower, adjusting his body to make her more comfortable.

She nestled against him and pretended to sleep but she never drifted off again. She didn't want to miss a minute of being held in his arms. Suspended between the past and the future, she cherished the long miles and wished, just for a little while, that their journey never had to end.

After a while, Samson pulled off the highway and said, "This is our motel."

She sat up reluctantly, missing Gideon's warmth and the tenderness of his touch. As she stepped out of the car, the smells and sounds of a strange city surrounded her. She was far from everything she'd ever known.

Tomorrow could start a new phase of her life or leave her forever in darkness. Either way, she realized that she wanted one person beside her as she moved into the uncertain future. She wanted Gideon Troyer in her life.

Rebecca's frayed nerves kept her from enjoying even Gideon's company as they rode in a taxi toward the clinic the morning of her surgery. Samson preferred not to drive into the crowded streets of the city. He remained at the motel outside of the city to take them home the day after tomorrow.

This is it. It's going to happen today.

Gideon and Vera kept up a lighthearted conversation about the sights they were passing, but Rebecca remained silent. What if the surgery succeeded? What if it failed? The possibilities ran around and around in her head like a kitten chasing its own tail.

At the clinic, she went inside holding on to her aunt's arm with a hand that trembled. For a second, she wondered if her knees would support her.

"Relax," Gideon said quietly. "It's going to be all right."

Vera said, “I pray God hears your words.”

When they stopped, Rebecca asked, “Is this it?”

“It’s the elevator,” Gideon replied.

A ding sounded. Rebecca felt the rush of people moving past them. Gideon spoke from behind her. “Dr. Tuva Eriksson is on the fourteenth floor.”

When the crowd departed, her aunt led her forward and then turned around.

“I have heard of these contraptions but I’ve never been in one.” Vera’s voice sounded as shaky as Rebecca felt.

Rebecca noted a faint sensation of movement as the elevator rose. Twice it stopped with a slight jerk and more people got on. Finally, Gideon said, “This is our floor.”

Vera moved forward, forcing Rebecca to follow. A few steps later, they entered what she assumed was the doctor’s waiting room. A cheerful woman’s voice greeted them and presented them with forms to fill out.

Vera said, “Why don’t you sit down, child?”

Gideon took hold of her hand. “This way.”

He led her to a chair and took a seat beside her across the room. Quietly, he asked, “Are you nervous? Don’t be. It is in God’s hands.” He covered her clenched fingers with his large warm hand.

“I know that whatever happens is His will. I must accept this.”

“I’ve been wearing out my knees praying for you.”

She grinned at that. “Your knees will recover. Prayer is *goot* for you.”

“You are *goot* for me, too. You make me want to be a better man.”

“Can Vera hear us?”

“No, she’s talking to the nurse. Why?”

“About what you said the other day.”

“I’ve said a lot of things.”

“The thing you asked me to think about.” Was he going to make this difficult?

“Oh, that I want to marry you.”

The teasing tone of his words made her relax. “Have you changed your mind?”

“Not in the least. I want it with all my heart.”

She had to be sure. “You wish to marry me even if this surgery fails?”

“Even then. I love you, Rebecca Beachy. I can’t imagine my life without you in it.”

What was she waiting for? She’d been alone for ten years because she had been afraid he wouldn’t want her with her handicap, afraid she didn’t deserve happiness with him. Now, he was offering her the love she had turned down and regretted for all these years.

She drew a deep breath. “I want you to know that I love you, too, Gideon Troyer.”

“You do?” His shocked surprise made her smile.

From across the room a woman’s voice called out, “Rebecca Beachy, we’re ready for you.”

* * *

She loved him!

Gideon was forced to wait quietly as Rebecca was led away when what he wanted to do was throw his arms around her and kiss her breathless.

He'd never been happier. He'd never been more terrified.

Vera sat down beside him. "Your presence has been a great comfort to me, Gideon. I'm glad my father suggested that you come."

"I'm happy to help. Rebecca has always been dear to me."

"So I gathered," she said with a sympathetic smile.

He wanted to share his good news but he knew that would be up to Rebecca. "I want only what is best for her."

"As do I, but her fate is up to God." Vera clasped her hands together, closed her eyes and bowed her head.

Gideon knew she was praying. He closed his eyes and did the same.

Fifteen minutes later, the same nurse came to the doorway and spoke to them. "You can come back for a few minutes. The doctor would like to talk to all of you."

Gideon jumped to his feet to follow her down a short hallway. They entered a darkened room. Rebecca lay on a bed with the sheets drawn up to her chin and a pale blue surgical bonnet covering her hair.

Vera took her hand. "How are you doing?"

"*Goot.* Is Gideon here?"

"*Ja,* I'm right here." He wanted to hold her in his arms but had to settle for touching her cheek.

As he stood beside Rebecca, the doctor came into the room. "Good morning, Miss Beachy. I'm Dr. Tuva Eriksson. I'll be doing your surgery today. The surgery itself will take approximately two hours. During that time, I'll separate your iris, the colored part of your eye, from the lens behind it. Because of your uveitus, your lens is opaque and hardened. I'll use an ultrasound probe to liquefy the damaged lens and extract it. Then I'll replace your lens with an acrylic prosthetic lens. Are you with me so far?"

Rebecca nodded. "I understand."

"Once the surgery is finished, your eyes will be covered with gauze and special hard eye patches to prevent you from accidentally injuring them. Tomorrow morning, I'll have you come to my office and we'll remove the bandages there. Any questions?"

She shook her head. "No. I wanted to thank you for waiving your fee. That was very kind of you."

"When Dr. Philip White explained that the Amish live without medical insurance and how they collectively pay for the cost of such care when it is needed, I had to help. You must understand this may not be successful, that the damage inside your eye may be too severe to allow vision even with a new lens."

"I do."

"All right. I've got to go scrub in. You may say goodbye to your family, and the nurse will take you back to the O.R."

Gideon thanked the doctor and waited as Vera kissed Rebecca's cheek and left the room. When they were alone, he bent and kissed her lips. "Be brave, my love."

"I'm so scared."

"I know. I am, too. But courage is simply fear that has said its prayers." The nurse came back into the room and he was forced to leave. Out in the waiting room, he prayed as he had never prayed before.

Three hours later, Dr. Eriksson came in with a smile on her face. "It went well, and she is in recovery."

"Can she see?" Gideon asked.

"We won't know that until we take her dressings off tomorrow, but I'm hopeful. There was less scarring than I feared. She should be ready to be released in half an hour. Make sure she gets lots of rest. Tomorrow will be a big day for all of us."

Chapter Fourteen

The following morning, Gideon called for a cab and waited impatiently outside Rebecca and Vera's motel room. When the car pulled up, Gideon knocked on Rebecca's door. It opened almost instantly. He saw Rebecca's pale face and he wanted to pull her into his arms and kiss her.

Instead, he said, "The taxi is waiting."

She merely nodded. Her bottom lip was clenched between her teeth but he saw the tremor she was trying to hide. She was scared. He would be, too, if he were in her shoes. When he helped her into the backseat of the cab, he asked, "Bad night?"

"I didn't sleep much. My eyes feel as if they are full of sand."

"The doctor said to expect that."

"I know, but it doesn't make it easy to endure."

Vera came out of the room. "I miss my own bed. I will be glad to get home."

Gideon moved aside as Vera climbed in, then took a seat beside her. No one said what he knew they were all thinking. In a few minutes, they would know if Rebecca could see.

He thought of all he'd given up to have her reach this point. He'd given up his business and friends. He'd given up the very thing he loved most besides Rebecca. Flying. If it wasn't enough, he'd give up his arms and his legs if the Lord asked it of him, if only she could be made whole.

They made the ride to the eye clinic in silence. Looking over at his companions, Gideon saw Vera had her eyes closed, but her lips were moving in silent prayer. He added his own silent pleas for Rebecca's recovery.

At the clinic they took the elevator to the fourteenth floor but today they didn't have to wait to see the doctor. As soon as they arrived they were ushered into an exam room. The cheerful nursing staff expressed their well wishes and then Dr. Eriksson walked in.

"Dim the lights, please."

The nurse by the door lowered the lights. Gideon's pulse shot up. *Please, God, let her see.*

Dr. Eriksson said, "Rebecca, I'm going to take the eye patches off first."

After the cupped protectors were removed, there were only two small gauze pads taped to Rebecca's face.

"All right, I'm taking the gauze off now." The doctor peeled back the strips of tape that held them in place and the dressings fell away.

Rebecca sat with her eyes closed and her hands clenched together in her lap. Her knuckles stood out white against the blue of her dress.

"Open your eyes when you're ready," the doctor coaxed.

"I can't."

"Yes, you can." Gideon dropped to one knee in front of her and took her hand.

She squeezed his fingers. "I'm afraid."

"We can bear all things by the grace of God."

"By the grace of God," she whispered. Taking a deep breath, she opened her eyes.

Light stabbed into Rebecca's eyes. She pressed them closed against the foreign sensation. She squinted through one eye. Colors and shapes began to form. Elation made her draw a quick breath.

A woman in a white coat stood in front of her. This must be the doctor through whose hands God had worked a miracle. Her Aunt Vera, looking so much older than she remembered, stood at her side. Her hands were clasped together in front of her mouth. A man dressed in plain clothes knelt before her. Her long-lost love. Gideon Troyer had matured from a boy into a ruggedly handsome man. His face was filled with hope and worry and love.

Everything blurred as tears filled her eyes and ran down her cheeks. She began to sob.

Gideon pressed her hands in a tight grip. "It's all right, love. It's all right. I'm so sorry. We can bear this together."

Rebecca blinked to clear her vision. There were tears on Gideon's cheek, too. Gently, she stretched out her fingers and brushed them away. "Don't cry."

Wonder filled his voice. "How do you know I'm crying?"

"I see your tears."

"You see them? You can see?" Joy bloomed in his eyes. His wonderful, beautiful eyes.

"Yes, I can."

Overcome, he bowed his head and covered his face with his hands. She looked down in wonder at her dress. "I'm wearing blue. I always thought this dress was dark blue, but it's not. It's indigo blue." She looked at her fingers and down at her shoes as she wiggled them.

She looked up at the nurses standing near the door. They all wore colorful uniforms. "I see red flowers and a rainbow and an eye chart. I see the big *E*. I can see all of the letters, even the small ones. I can see everything."

Rebecca grasped the hand of Dr. Eriksson. "Thank you. Thank you so much."

Smiling, Dr. Eriksson said, "I am happy we have succeeded."

Vera rushed forward and engulfed Rebecca in a bear hug as the nurses clapped and cheered. Gideon rose and stepped back but he was smiling, too. Finally, Dr. Eriksson called for quiet. "There is someone waiting to hear your news, Rebecca. Let me get him on the phone."

Rebecca pulled back from her aunt's embrace to gaze at the face of the woman who'd given her a home for so many years. "*Aenti* Vera, your *kapp* is on crooked."

"So is yours," Gideon said, reaching to pull it straight by the ties that hung beside her cheeks. The knuckles of his hands brushed her face in a sweet, soft caress. Quietly he said, "Your *kapp* is on straight. There's no egg yolk from breakfast on your dress, no dust from the buggy seat on your behind. You look lovely."

She tipped her head to the side. "Have you said that to me before?"

An odd look flitted across his face and was gone. "I don't think I have."

"Funny, I seem to remember someone saying it."

Dr. Eriksson interrupted her. "Rebecca, I'm putting this caller on speaker phone so everyone can hear."

"Rebecca? Is that you?" It was her grandfather. In the background she heard the sound of Amish voices singing hymns.

"*Ja, Daadi,* it's me."

She waited but he didn't speak again. Instead, she heard Dr. White. "Quiet, everyone. Quiet, please. Rebecca, many of your family and friends have gathered here in the medical clinic to await your news this morning."

Her heart turned over with happiness when she realized how much everyone cared. "Then I won't keep them in suspense any longer. God has been merciful. I can see."

The sounds of happy chatter, laughter and praises to God's goodness filled the air. Rebecca closed her eyes to listen to each voice. She heard Emma's happy squeal and Sarah's voice. Even Faith was there along with so many others who called out their well wishes.

Vera moved closer to the phone. "We will be home late tonight, but on Sunday we will see all of you at the preaching at Adrian Lapp's farm. Bless you for your thoughts and prayers."

"I will be there," her grandfather said with a catch in his voice.

Rebecca squeezed her aunt's hand. "I can't wait to see each and every one of you. Goodbye for now."

"God speed you safely home," her grandfather called out. Dr. Eriksson pushed a button and the phone when silent.

Rebecca rose and turned to Gideon, wobbling slightly as she struggled to keep her balance in her newly sighted world. "I want to go outside. I want to see the sky."

"Before you go, I want you to take this card." Dr. Eriksson handed one to Vera and to Rebecca. "I am leaving for Sweden on Christmas Day. Until then, anything that you need, don't hesitate to call me. If you have any trouble with your vision, I want to know about it. This surgery is in the early experimental stages. There may be side effects we haven't encountered yet. After I leave, you can contact Dr. Barbara Kennedy. Her number is also on the card. She is familiar with my work, and she will be happy to follow you. The nurse is going to give you some eye drops. I want you to use them exactly as I have prescribed."

Rebecca accepted the small bottles and listened to the instructions from the nurse. When the woman was finished, Rebecca spoke to the doctor again. "I will take good care of my eyes, I promise. I don't have the words to thank you for all you have done."

"It was my pleasure, Rebecca. I wish you the best of luck in the future."

Eager to be outside, Rebecca headed for the door with Vera and Gideon right behind her. The second she stepped into the hallway she stopped. The walls and the floor seemed to be rushing at her. She closed her eyes to regain her balance.

Gideon said, "What's wrong?"

She blew out a hollow breath. "I reckon I need to go slower."

"Take my arm." He offered his elbow.

Grateful, she held on to him and they started forward. The rushing sensation became too much; she closed her eyes and followed him trustingly.

When the cold air hit her face she knew they were outside. She opened her eyes and looked up. Steel, glass and concrete towers leaned over her. The tall buildings blocked much of the sky. It was like being at the bottom of a deep well.

Gideon must have sensed her disappointment. "You will see the sky soon enough when we leave the city."

She glanced at his face, taking in each of his features in turn, his broad forehead and strong brows, his wide blue eyes and handsome lips that she wanted to kiss. Reaching out, she touched a scar in his eyebrow. "I remember when you got this."

"I fell sliding into home plate at school."

She touched his chin. "This one I don't remember."

He rubbed it. "I got this one from a propeller before I learned to watch where I was walking around planes."

"You've changed so much from what I remember."

"Have I? You haven't changed at all."

"I doubt that. I'm almost afraid to look in a mirror."

"I still see the prettiest girl in Berlin, Ohio."

He started walking toward the taxi stand. She

closed her eyes and shook her head. "This is hard to get used to."

"Then keep your eyes closed for a while. I'll take care of you."

She squeezed his arm. "I know you will."

The car ride home was like a trip through a magical wonderland. Rebecca couldn't get enough of the sights flying past her window. She wanted to see everything, but it wasn't long before her eyes began to ache and burn. At Gideon's insistence, she put on her dark glasses and tried to rest.

Like a reluctant toddler, she fought the weariness dragging at her mind and body. Each time she closed her eyes she was afraid her vision would be gone when she opened them again. Finally, she fell asleep as the car headed westward. She dreamed she was flying. She woke in complete darkness and cried out in fear.

"It's okay." Gideon spoke softly to her.

She clutched his hand. "Everything has gone black."

"That's because it is nighttime." Gradually, his face came into focus.

"How long have I been asleep?"

"Hours. We're almost home. You've been worn out with worry and lack of sleep. I almost didn't have the heart to wake you, but it's time for your eye drops."

She accepted the small vials from his hands, put

her head back and blinked at the sting of the liquid hitting her eyes. After wiping away the excess, she glanced at the front seat where Vera dozed, too. "You have taken good care of us, Gideon."

"I will always take good care of you, Rebecca." He kissed her forehead.

It wasn't enough for her. She raised her face to his and drew him close. His kiss, tender and tentative at first, quickly deepened with passion. His firm lips sparked an ardent answering need in her that left her breathless. When he pulled away she sensed his reluctance to let her go.

"I love you, Rebecca Beachy," he whispered in her ear.

"And I you."

He kissed her once more and she settled against his side, more content than she'd been for ten years. God had been good to her.

Chapter Fifteen

The first week Rebecca was home, a constant stream of visitors kept her busy. She made a game of trying to guess who her visitors were before they spoke. Emma she guessed because she was with Adam. Sarah, she didn't know until she heard her voice. Faith she guessed because she walked with a slight limp.

Rebecca wrote the first of several lengthy letters to Grace and was delighted when a reply arrived a few days later. She left the letter lying on the kitchen table when her parents and her grandfather were visiting. It disappeared a short time later and she knew her mother had taken it to read.

Perhaps in time, God would show them a way to heal the breach in the family. Until then, she was happy to serve as a bridge between Grace and the rest of the family.

What Rebecca missed was seeing Gideon every

day, but she understood that he had work to do, both for Adam and at his new home. As Christmas drew closer, she grew used to her restored vision. The only time she found she had to keep her eyes closed was when she tried to quilt. Her fingers knew what to do. Her eyes only served to mess her up.

When Sunday finally arrived, Rebecca traveled to Adrian Lapp's farm with a happy heart. She had so much to be thankful for. She looked forward to lifting her voice in song praising God's mercy and love.

As her aunt drove the buggy down the highway, Rebecca paid careful attention to the route. Soon, she would try driving again. Gideon's new home was on the farm adjacent to the Lapps' property. When his house came into view, she craned her neck to see it. It was small by Amish standards but it had a pretty front porch. The barn was in need of some repairs. He had spoken about love but not about marriage; still she found it exciting to imagine living there with Gideon if they were wed one day.

What was the inside of the house like? She owned a few pieces of furniture. Was there room for her special things, or had Gideon brought a houseful of furniture with him? What she wouldn't give to turn down the lane this minute and see his home. She didn't bother suggesting it for Vera was in a hurry.

She would have to wait until Christmas for Gideon to show her around the place.

The minute they reached the Lapp farm, Gideon sought them out and Rebecca's heart skipped with happiness at the sight of his face. He offered to unhitch their horse and to help carry their baskets of food to the house. Vera smiled at him and walked off to speak with her friends leaving the two of them alone for a few minutes. Bless Aunt Vera for her understanding of young hearts.

"I've missed you," he said as he set to work on the harness.

A sweet thrill raced through her. "I've missed you, too."

"Are things getting back to normal?"

Pulling her coat tight against the cold, she raised her face to the heavens. "I can see the sky, Gideon. I see the birds in the air. I see the snow-blanketed fields waiting for the warm sun of spring to awaken them. My life will never be normal. It can only be miraculous."

He smiled at her. "I'm happy for you."

She giggled. "I'm happy for me, too."

He sobered and said, "There are some things we need to discuss, Rebecca."

"What things?"

"There are things about my past you need to hear."

Another buggy drove in and stopped beside them.

As the family climbed out, Rebecca heard Katie Sutter calling her name. She waved and turned back to Gideon. "What did you wish to tell me?"

"It can wait. Go and visit with your friends."

She lingered knowing Katie would wait. "Tomorrow is Christmas Eve. Is your family coming?"

"Not until Christmas Day, thank goodness. My house is a wreck. I've got to get some cleaning done before my mother arrives. Do you know of a girl who might want to earn some extra wages?"

This was her chance to do Gideon a favor after all he had done for her. "I know just the person."

"Really? Do you think she could come tomorrow?"

"I'm sure of it."

"Great. I've got a job tomorrow morning in Sugarcreek, but I should be home by ten o'clock."

"Write out a list of things you want done and leave it on the table. You can settle up her wages when you get back."

"That's one less thing I have to worry about."

"I'm glad I could help." She patted the horse as he led the mare away. Joining Katie who was waiting for her, Rebecca went into the house to get ready for worship.

Early the next morning, she took her aunt's horse and buggy and drove for the first time since recovering her sight. It was scary, but when Gideon's house came into view, her spirits soared.

True to her suggestion, he'd made a list of things to be cleaned. Rolling up her sleeves, she set to work in the kitchen and thought about the meals she might one day make here. The morning passed quickly as she cleaned and dusted the furniture in the living room, aired out the sheets in the guest rooms and put a shine on the linoleum floor of the bathroom. It was past ten before she was done with Gideon's list and the extra things she found on her own.

After taking a short break to have a cup of coffee, she couldn't resist a peek into the one room Gideon didn't have on his cleaning list. His bedroom.

She eased open the door and smiled. Gideon wasn't a slob. The room and its contents were neat enough. His clothes hung from pegs on the wall. A straw hat for summer sat on top of the bureau along with a comb and brush. The plank floor was bare except for a rag rug at the side of the bed. A beautiful star-patterned quilt covered the bed itself in shades of gold, greens and muted reds.

She blushed at the thought of lying beneath the quilt in Gideon's arms. If their love was real and they took the next step in their relationship, this was where she would spend her wedding night, where her children, if they were so blessed, would be born. She ran her hand over the workmanship of the quilt and admired the fine stitching.

As her fingers traced the pattern of the squares

and triangles they seemed familiar. She closed her eyes. Her heart started pounding. It wasn't possible. How could Gideon own one of her quilts?

She kept her eyes closed and with trembling fingers, she searched for the corner block, the last block sewn. Relief made her knees weak when she found nothing in the first corner. There was no earthly reason for this quilt to be the one she had given to Booker, yet it felt so familiar. She had worked for weeks on one just like this.

She moved to the foot of the bed and untucked the second corner and then the third. Still nothing.

It was just a quilt. Most likely his mother had made it for him. At the top of the bed, she folded back the last corner. When she did, her fingers brushed crossed the tiny rows of dots. Dots of Braille that spelled her name and the date she had finished her work. November 2.

How was this possible? Booker had said he would treasure it forever. Could he have sold it or given it to Gideon? Did they know each other?

Another possibility took the strength from her legs. Rebecca sank onto the bed. From the moment she met Booker there had been something familiar about him. It was as if she had known him forever. Booker was a pilot as Gideon had been. Gideon returned home only weeks after she said goodbye to Booker.

If only we'd met in another time and another place.

She recalled Booker's whisper and the touch of his fingers on her cheek.

Please, God, I don't want to believe that he lied to me, that he played some kind of game at my expense.

From outside, she heard Gideon calling hello. She couldn't answer. She remained on the bed, hands folded, praying there was a logical explanation.

The door opened and Gideon poked his head in. "I saw your buggy outside. What are you doing here? The house looks great, by the way. Where is your cleaning girl?"

"I'm the cleaning girl. I've been admiring your quilt, Gideon. The craftsmanship is very good. Where did you get it?"

He didn't say anything, but she saw the change come over his face and she knew. Her heart sank. "All this time, I thought I'd given it to a friend."

"You did." He crossed the room and sank to his knees beside her.

She shook her head. "How you must have laughed at the blind woman stumbling around. It must have seemed so funny that I didn't recognize the man I once planned to marry. Did you really have a cold or was that an act? You did a great job. I never suspected it was you."

"I wasn't laughing at you, Rebecca. I was getting to know a remarkable woman who was forbidden to me. Please, let me explain."

"You've had weeks to explain yourself. You deceived me. You lied." She stood and tried to walk past him but he grabbed her arm.

"I didn't tell you I was Booker because he no longer exists. I gave up that life. I knew I could never have you unless I did."

"And the money for my surgery, that came from you, too?" A headache began pandering behind her eyes.

"Yes."

"I should be grateful for that. I am grateful, but I can't love a man who has deceived me to such a degree."

"I was under the ban when I bid on your quilt. I was afraid you wouldn't use the money if you knew it was from me. I didn't tell you about the money because I didn't want your gratitude. I wanted you to love me, to love Gideon Troyer, an Amish handyman, not Booker, the man who gave you back your sight."

She stared at his hand until he let go of her arm. "I did love Gideon Troyer, Amish handyman. Sadly, he isn't what he claims to be."

Gideon raked his fingers through his hair. "That's not true. This is who I am now. I promise you, this is the truth. I believe God brought me to my senses and brought me home so that I could devote my life to loving you. I know I was wrong to keep it a secret. I should have had the courage to tell you the truth, but I was afraid. Forgive me, Rebecca. I'll do anything to make this up to you."

"You are forgiven, Gideon. But I never want to see you again."

She fled from the room and rushed down the steps of his home toward the buggy waiting in the yard. She heard him calling her name, heard his footsteps pounding after her. Tears blurred her vision and streamed down her face. She never saw the rock she stumbled over. She fell, striking her head with sickening pain against the buggy wheel.

"Rebecca? Rebecca, darling, are you all right?"

She felt his hands on her shoulders as he gently lifted her. Pain sent flashes of light lancing through her skull.

"You're bleeding. Hold still."

She raised a hand to her forehead and felt it come away sticky. The smell of blood filled her nostrils. She opened her eyes and a scream ripped from her throat.

Gideon pulled a kerchief from his pocket and pressed it against the gash on Rebecca's head. "It's all right. You're going to be all right."

"No, no, no." She began sobbing uncontrollably.

Sitting in the snow beside her, he tried to soothe her. "Head wounds bleed a lot, but it's not as bad as you think."

"I'm sorry. I'm so sorry," she muttered as she grabbed the front of his coat.

"It's all right. Do you think you can stand?"

He helped her to her feet but she kept her death grip on his jacket. Her eyes were wide with shock. Tears flowed down her face unchecked.

He gathered her close. This was his fault. He should have found the courage to confess his deception weeks ago. He never should have asked for her love until everything was out in the open.

He disengaged her fingers and put his kerchief in her hand. "Keep this pressed against the cut. I think the bleeding has slowed."

She took his kerchief with trembling fingers and pressed it to her forehead. All the color was gone from her face. He wasn't sure she could stand unaided. Her prayer *kapp* had come off. He bent down to pick it up and held out her. "Here is your *kapp*."

She stretched out her free hand—six inches to the side of his. Her eyes were unfocused and staring.

Icy fear poured through his body. "Rebecca, what's wrong?"

"I can't see, Gideon. I'm blind."

No, please God, not after all she had endured.

He scooped her up and placed her in the buggy. "I'm taking you to the doctor."

She trembled on the bench. "It won't matter."

Gideon raced around the other side and climbed in. He gathered the reins and wrapped one arm around Rebecca. He slapped the reins against the horse's rump, setting the animal in motion. Once they reached the highway, he urged the animal to a faster pace.

It was reckless driving at such a speed with only one hand holding the lines, but he didn't dare let go of Rebecca as she slumped against him. She was so pale. There didn't seem to be any strength in her body.

Please God, why are You doing this? Don't leave her blind. She doesn't deserve this. Take my sight instead, I beg You.

The trip into Hope Springs seemed to take forever. Finally, they hit Main Street. Heads turned as people stared at his breakneck speed through town.

One more corner. If he didn't overturn them here the medical clinic was on the next block. His wheels skidded on the snow-covered street as Vera's mare made the turn. The buggy stayed upright. Gideon hauled her to a sliding stop when they reached the front of the building.

"We're here, Rebecca. Dr. White is going to fix you up. Don't worry about a thing." He was babbling, but he didn't care. He helped her out of the buggy and gently led her to the clinic door.

Please, God, let her be okay.

Inside, he gave a hurried explanation to the receptionist. Moments later, Amber and Dr. White came out and took Rebecca with them to the exam room.

Gideon sank down on the waiting-room chair and stared at his hands. They were stained with blood. Folding them tightly together, he began to pray.

Twenty minutes later, Dr. White came to the doorway and motioned for Gideon to come with him. Gideon followed the doctor to his office. Impatiently, he asked, "How is she?"

Dr. White opened his door. "Please sit down."

When Gideon entered, he saw Rebecca already seated in a chair in front of the doctor's desk. Gideon took the empty seat beside her.

He wanted to take her hand, reassure himself that she was okay, but he could tell from the frozen look on her face that she wouldn't welcome the gesture. The doctor took a seat behind the desk and faced them.

Gideon braced himself to hear what he feared most.

The doctor steepled his fingers together. "The blow to Rebecca's head doesn't seem to be serious. I can't find a physical reason for her blindness. I see no signs of hemorrhage in her eyes, no evidence of detached retina. Frankly, I'm stumped."

Rebecca said, "I have a bad migraine right now."

The weight of worry made it hard for Gideon to draw a breath. "Is this permanent?"

Dr. White met Gideon's gaze. "I can't say for sure. In light of her recent surgery, I put a call in to Dr. Eriksson. She's concerned there may be a complication from the surgery that is unrelated to this bump on the head. She feels it's imperative that she see Rebecca as soon as possible."

Puzzled, Gideon said, "I thought she was leaving the country?"

"She is. Tomorrow morning. She wants to see Rebecca today. She suggested she be flown via an air ambulance to New York this afternoon."

Gideon glanced from Rebecca's stoic face to Dr. White's concerned one. "Why do I hear a 'but' coming?"

"Rebecca's condition doesn't meet the urgent care criteria for an air ambulance."

Gideon couldn't believe what he was hearing. "You've got to be kidding! She struck her head and went blind. That's not urgent?"

"We're not sending her to a hospital for intensive care. We're sending her to an eye surgeon for an examination. It's a big difference to the air transport companies."

Gideon nodded. "What are our other options?"

"We can contact a private air ambulance company, but it will be very costly, and they may not be available on such short notice."

"Can we get a commercial flight from Akron or Cleveland?" Gideon wasn't going to sit still and do nothing.

"I may have a better option. I've contacted a friend of mine who owns a small plane. He's in L.A.

on business, but his wife has agreed to let us use the plane. I understand you're a pilot, Mr. Troyer. Can you fly a Piper Cub?"

Finally, a solution. "Yes."

"No," Rebecca said just as quickly.

Gideon glanced at her face and felt his blood turning to sludge that barely moved through his veins. "You don't mean that."

"You told me that Booker is gone. You promised me. You are an Amish handyman, Gideon Troyer. You cannot fly a plane. I cannot ride in a plane. It is against the *Ordnung* of our church."

Dr. White said gently, "Rebecca, you can fly if Bishop Zook gives you permission. It will only take a few minutes for Amber to fetch him from his farm."

"But he cannot give Gideon permission to pilot the plane."

The doctor said, "This may be a case where it is better to ask forgiveness than permission."

Gideon swallowed hard. He had the knowledge and the power that might save Rebecca's sight. If he used that knowledge and went against the teachings of their church, he would lose her love.

He slipped from his chair to kneel beside her and took her hand between his own. "I love you with all my heart, Rebecca. If it is God's will that you never see again, it changes nothing. But, I beg you, don't make me stand by helplessly when I can save you."

She stared straight ahead as a single tear rolled down her cheek. “A vow cannot be discarded because it is inconvenient, my love.”

“Please, Rebecca.” His voice broke as his heart shattered into tiny bits.

“You promised. Did you mean it?” she whispered.

That he held true to his vow meant more to her than her sight. He would never disappoint her again. “I did.”

He laid his head in her lap. A sob broke free from him and then another. He barely felt the comfort of her hand stroking his hair.

Chapter Sixteen

After a few minutes, Gideon stood and wiped the tears from his face with the back of his sleeve. "I will not break my vows again, but I can't stand by and do nothing."

Rebecca said, "We must leave this in God's hands."

"If I can be the instrument of your blindness, I can be the instrument He uses to heal you—within the rules of the *Ordnung*. I'm not the only one who can fly a plane. Dr. White, may I use your phone?"

"Certainly." The doctor handed him the receiver.

Gideon dialed the number of his old business. He felt his spirits rise when Roseanne answered the phone. He said, "Roseanne, it's Gideon."

"It's about time you called. We've been feeling neglected."

"I'm sorry. I'd love to chat but I need to speak to Craig. It's important."

"He's on the runway with the young couple who

are about to take a sightseeing tour of the lakes for their honeymoon. I can patch him through to you if you would like."

"That would be great." Gideon waited impatiently until Craig came on the line.

"Booker, is that you? How's the Amish life treating you?"

"Let's just say it has its challenges as well as its rewards." Gideon squeezed Rebecca's hand. She gripped his fingers tightly in return.

"What can I do for you?"

"I need you to fly someone from Hope Springs to New York today."

"Seriously?"

"I've never been more serious in my life. She's very important to me, and she needs to see an eye specialist as soon as possible. I need your help, buddy."

"Okay. Hang on just a second. Mr. and Mrs. Weaver, I'm sorry but I'm going to have to cancel your tour today. I'm having some technical difficulties. Don't worry, you'll get a full refund and we can reschedule any time that is convenient for you at a ten-percent discount."

The sound of the plane powering down was followed by a rapid exchange of words Gideon couldn't understand. He heard the plane doors open and slam shut again. After a few minutes, Craig came back on the phone. "Okay, where's the closest airport?"

Gideon said, "Craig, you didn't have to lie for me."

His friend chuckled. "Booker, I didn't lie. It would be technically difficult to come get your friend with these people on board. Think of the fuel consumption."

"I'll never be able to repay you for this."

"Just tell me where to land."

Gideon gave the phone to Dr. White. He, in turn, gave Craig the location of the private airstrip. When he was done relaying the information, Dr. White handed the phone back to Gideon.

"Thanks, Craig. You're the best." Gideon knew words could not convey his gratitude.

"I know it. See you in a little over an hour."

After hanging up the phone, Gideon looked to Dr. White. "We should get Bishop Zook here. Rebecca won't go, I won't take her, unless he gives his permission."

"I understand." The doctor left the room.

Gideon took a seat beside Rebecca again. He grasped her cold hands. "Don't worry. Everything will be fine."

She didn't speak. Not when the bishop arrived and gave his blessing for the trip. Not when Amber drove them to the airfield, not even when Gideon helped her into the plane and snapped her seat belt closed.

She had retreated to somewhere he couldn't follow. He wasn't sure she would ever come back to him.

* * *

Rebecca blinked as the drops hit her eyes. She hated this part. The drops always burned. Her headache was unbearable. Her stomach churned with nausea.

"Try to relax," the nurse said. "Dr. Eriksson will be in soon. Call if you need anything." She pressed a buzzer into Rebecca's hand. The sound of the door closing signaled that she had left the room.

"How are you feeling?" Gideon asked, his voice thick with emotion.

She couldn't believe she hadn't realized who Booker really was. She had been blind in more ways than one. "My head is splitting."

"I wish I could help."

"I know you do. I have only myself to blame. Pride sent me running away from you."

He took her hand and she squeezed his fingers. He said, "We are a well-matched pair, then. It was pride that sent me running away years ago. It was stubbornness and pride that kept me away."

"Bishop Zook says all men must battle false pride. He says none of us are truly humble before God, but that we must strive always for that humility. It is only by being humble that we can hear God's voice."

"I need you to help keep me on the right path."

"As I need you. Don't think this is your fault."

"How can I not?"

"You don't have the power to take away my sight

any more than you have the power to restore it. There is a lesson for us in this. We must seek God's help to understand what He wishes us to learn."

"I've learned I will never keep a secret from you again."

"If we can't trust each other, we have nothing together."

"God has shown me the error of my ways. From this day forward I will never keep anything from you."

The door opened and Dr. Eriksson said, "Tell me what's going on. Rebecca, what kind of pain are you having?"

"I have a bad headache. I can't see anything."

"Is it like a migraine?"

"Ja."

"I want you to sit still. Mr. Troyer, help move her chair up to the table." Gideon did as the doctor asked.

"Good. Now, Rebecca, there is a chin rest in front of you. Can you feel it?"

"I do."

"Good. Put your chin on the rest and hold still. Try not to move your eyes. Stare straight ahead. I'm going to look into them and take some pictures."

Rebecca heard the sound of the shutter clicking. She followed the doctor's instructions. Once, she thought she caught a flicker of light, but it was gone so quickly she thought she had imagined it.

"You may sit back now," the doctor said.

"Can you tell us what's wrong?" Gideon asked.

"The surgical site looks fine. I'm happy to say there's no sign of infection or other serious medical complications."

"But she's blind."

"I saw several cases like this when I was in Australia. Rebecca, are you prone to car sickness or motion sickness?"

"I have been all my life."

"There is a rare syndrome called Footballer's Migraine. It's a severe migraine headache and visual impairment triggered by a blow to the head such as soccer players get when they head the ball. It's thought that dilation of the blood vessels in the brain puts pressure on the optic nerves."

"Is there a treatment?" Hope began to uncurl inside Rebecca.

"There is. I'm going to have the nurse give you an injection of sumatriptan. It should take care of the headache and visual impairment in an hour or two."

"Will it happen again?" Gideon asked.

"Avoiding blows to the head should keep it from reoccurring, but if it does, Dr. White will be able to administer the drug at his office."

A huge weight lifted from Gideon's chest. He squeezed Rebecca's hand. "That's wonderful news."

"If it doesn't work, I suggest Rebecca enter the

hospital and undergo a CT and MRI of the head to rule out other causes as soon as possible."

"I'll see that she does," Gideon promised.

"I know this has given you both a fright, but I'm thankful that I'm not seeing any complications from the surgery. The nurse will be in a few minutes. Try to relax, Rebecca. It's going to be fine. I'm going to cover your eyes with gauze pads just to keep the light out of them. Leave them on until your headache is completely gone."

"Thank you, Doctor," she muttered.

Once Dr. Eriksson was out of the room, Gideon cupped Rebecca's face in his hands and kissed her cheeks. "Did you hear? You're going to be fine."

"Maybe." Her voice was weak.

He knew better than to ask if she loved him. She was in pain. All he wanted was for her to feel better. The future would take care of itself.

The nurse came in and gave Rebecca a shot in her arm. After that, they were free to go. He led her out of the eye clinic and onto the crowded sidewalk. Christmas shoppers were out in droves this final day before the holiday.

Rebecca pressed close to his side. She didn't like crowds, didn't like to be jostled. He managed to flag down a taxi and gave the address of the airport where Craig was waiting for them. Christmas music blared from the car's radio.

Gideon spoke to the driver. "Could you turn the music down, please?"

Annoyed, the fellow said, "What? You Amish don't celebrate Christmas?"

"We do, but this young woman has a bad headache and loud sounds make it worse."

"Oh, sure. Sorry." The driver snapped the radio off.

"Danki," Rebecca murmured.

"What's that?" the cabbie asked as he pulled away.

"It means 'thank you,'" Gideon replied.

"You folks speak Dutch, don't you? My grandmother came from Holland."

"People call it Pennsylvania Dutch, but it's really Pennsylvania *Deitsch,* a German dialect," Gideon explained.

"Huh. I learn something new every day."

Thankfully, the man fell silent and Gideon was able to concentrate on Rebecca. Quietly, he asked, "Is the medicine helping?"

"*Nee.* Not yet."

"It will." It had to. It broke his heart to see her suffering.

When they reached the small airport at the outskirts of the city, Gideon paid the taxi driver and helped Rebecca to the plane where Craig was waiting for them.

"What's the verdict?" he asked.

Gideon said, "The doctor thinks it's temporary."

"Hey, that's great news."

It was great news if it were true. Gideon clung to his faith and prayed God would grant her a complete recovery as he helped her into the plane.

They had been in the air for nearly an hour when Rebecca's headache lessened and she noticed a faint crescent of light at the edge of the bandages over her eyes. Was her sight coming back?

Joy skipped across the surface of her heart the way a stone skips over the surface of a still pond and then settles into the depths. Carefully, she pushed the edge of the gauze pad upward.

The light increased. She closed her eyes tight and pulled the dressings off. If she opened her eyes would everything go dark again?

Have faith. Have faith, for God has chosen you to be one of His own.

Drawing a calming breath, she slowly opened her eyes. The tan leather grain of the seat in front of her came into focus. Above the seat, she saw the back of a man's head. His hair was short and blond. She was tempted to reach out and touch it just to assure herself that he was real.

She looked down at her hands clenched tightly together. Her vision suddenly blurred and fear shot through her until she realized it was her own tears making the world watery. Blinking them away, she glanced to the left.

Gideon sat beside her. His gaze was focused out the window beside him. He looked so tired. There were lines on his forehead and around his eyes that hadn't been there this morning. Had it only been this morning when she found the quilt? A lifetime had passed.

As she gazed at Gideon she wondered why she didn't recognize that Booker and he were the same person. His kindness, his sense of humor, the way his touch made her heart race, only one man could make her feel this way—as happy as thistledown on the wind.

They had faced a great test of their love and their faith and passed it. She had no idea what God had in store for her life, but each moment she had with Gideon would be a moment to treasure.

As though he sensed her eyes upon him, he looked in her direction. She smiled and said, "You look tired."

The range of emotions that crossed his face was priceless. It went from shock to hope to utter joy in the blink of an eye.

"You can see?" he whispered.

She could barely hear him over the drone of the airplane engine. "I can see how much you love me."

The relief on his face changed to deep thankfulness. "You don't need eyes for that. I promise you will always know how much I love you whether you can see me or not."

He leaned toward her until his lips brushed hers. Heady excitement rushed through her blood, leaving her dizzy. Her hands cupped his face as she deepened the kiss. How was it possible to love someone so much?

"You two are steaming up the windows!" Craig's voice penetrated Rebecca's haze of happiness.

"Mind your own business and keep your eyes toward the front, Law." Gideon smiled at Rebecca tenderly.

"You have such a beautiful smile." She would never grow tired of seeing it.

"I'm glad you like what you see."

How could she not? "I like the color of your eyes. I like the way your hair wants to curl over your ears. I love the way you look so Plain in those clothes. I could go on looking at you forever, Gideon Troyer."

Gideon gazed into her eyes. "That's what I had in mind. I love you, Rebecca, with all my heart and soul."

Craig said, "He's not much of a prize, Rebecca. You could do better."

Rebecca liked this English friend of Gideon's. She raised her voice so he could hear her. "I'm not so sure I could. He is a fine Amish man."

He glanced back at them and grinned. "I hope you know what you're getting into."

Gideon leaned over and kissed her. "Pay no attention to him."

She squeezed Gideon's hand, thankful and content to be near him, to see his face and read the love in his eyes. "So this is flying. I can see why you love it." Peering past him, she gasped at the sight. "The earth is so far away. Surely it would take us a day to fall so far."

Craig and Gideon laughed out loud. She blushed, knowing how foolish she must sound to these men of the air.

Gideon kissed her hand. "Let's hope we don't find out how long it takes, but with Murphy's Law at the controls, odds are anything can happen."

"Hey, I've only crashed one plane," Craig shot back.

Gideon brushed a wisp of hair back from Rebecca's face. "If I died today I would still be the happiest man on God's earth."

She gripped his hand. "I would rather be *down* on God's earth, but it is beautiful up here. You gave up so much to return to me. I'm sorry I doubted you. I will never doubt you again."

"I will never give you a reason to doubt my faith or my love. Flying is only one kind of freedom. The love we share is another, more potent kind. I've made the better trade."

"You say that now, but how will you feel in a year or ten years?"

"Rebecca, flying has always been my substitute

for you. I don't need a substitute any longer. Not if I have the real thing."

"I think I need to pinch myself and see if this is real."

"Go ahead. You'll find I'm real and really in love with you."

"God has truly blessed us, hasn't He?" She smiled at her beloved and read the answer in his eyes.

Chapter Seventeen

Gideon opened his eyes and stared at the ceiling of his bedroom. It was Christmas morning. The day the whole world celebrated the birth of the Christ Child. Rather than leave mankind to live in the darkness of sin, God sent His only son to bring light and forgiveness to all who would accept His gift.

Gideon rose from bed and dropped to his knees beside it. Bowing his head, he welcomed God's gift into his heart and gave thanks for the blessings in his life.

God willing, he and Rebecca would spend many Christmas mornings together with their children and grandchildren gathered around them. He prayed for her well-being as he wondered how she was doing after the adventures of yesterday.

Rising, he dressed quickly in the cold room and looked out the window. Fresh snow had fallen during the night, but the sun was shining on the horizon. It promised to be a beautiful day.

Down in the kitchen, he stoked the stove and brewed coffee. His family would be arriving in the early afternoon and there was much to be done.

He was finishing up his chores in the barn when he heard the bells of a sleigh coming up the lane. He looked out to see Rebecca guiding her horse toward the barn. Stepping out to meet her, he smiled as happiness poured through his veins. She was bundled up against the cold, but he'd never seen her look more beautiful.

"Merry Christmas. You must be frozen." He held out his arms to help her down.

"I am, but I'm sure you can find a way to warm me up." With a bright grin, she planted her hands on his shoulders as he grasped her slender waist.

He wasn't a man to turn from a challenge. He lifted her from her perch, but didn't set her feet on the snow. Instead, he held her against his chest, her face mere inches from his.

"Merry Christmas," she whispered before she slipped her arms around his neck and kissed him.

After a long moment, he lowered her to the ground but he didn't let her go. "How are you?"

She blew out a deep breath. "I'm a bit dizzy, but I don't think it has anything to do with my bump on the head."

He loved this lightness between them. "Are you saying I make your head spin?"

"And my heart, too."

"I don't have words to describe the way you make me feel, but I will spend a lifetime trying to make you understand how much I love you."

She pushed away slightly. "I look forward to that, but don't we have things to do?"

"*Ja,* we have much work to finish before my family arrives. Let me put your horse up and we can get started."

It took him only a few minutes to stable her mare. When he was finished, she asked, "What's first?"

"I thought we could gather some greenery for my mantel."

"Sounds like fun. Do you have a hatchet?"

He picked one up from his workbench near the barn door. "What self-respecting Amish handyman doesn't have a hatchet?"

"'Self-respecting.' That makes you sound so serious." She giggled and darted out the door.

Laughing, he chased after her. She was waiting with a snowball in hand. She let it fly and it smashed against his coat. He stumbled to a halt and held up his hand. "No. I refuse to throw snowballs at you."

She scooped up another handful and casually packed it together. "You don't have to throw any."

"Good. After what happened last time, I'm not taking that chance again."

"Fine. I'll do all the throwing." She let loose and knocked his hat from his head.

"Rebecca Marie Beachy, stop that." He bent to pick up his hat and felt a snowball hit his rear end. He straightened with as much dignity as he could muster, dusted off his hat and settled it on his head. He bent to scoop up a handful of snow and turned to face her.

Rebecca took a few steps back. "You said you weren't going to throw any at me."

"I can put snow down your collar without throwing it." He shifted his weapon from one hand to the other.

"Only if you can catch me." She took off toward the house at a run.

He caught up with her before she'd gone a dozen feet and swung her into his arms. She shrieked and squirmed, but he held on and turned her to face him. He gazed into her sparkling eyes and knew the joy that had been missing in his heart for a decade. "I love you."

"Not as much as I love you." She rose on tiptoe and planted a quick kiss on his lips.

Dropping back on her heels, she patted his chest. "Go cut the greenery. I've got to start baking the ham. Vera, Grandpa Reuben and his wife will be here soon. Adam and Emma are on their way, too."

Within the next two hours, Gideon's simple home came alive with the spirit of an Amish Christmas. The smell of pine boughs and food scented the air. Cookies, candy and snacks appeared on the countertops. His family arrived an hour after Rebecca's. The sounds of happy chatter and conversations filled the rooms as everyone became acquainted. Emma and Adam arrived shortly before three o'clock.

Gideon, his brothers and his nephews spent the afternoon trekking through the orchard to find the alpacas. Snow clung to the animals' thick coats and long eyelashes as they munched on hay bales Gideon had set out for them that morning. Afterward, the boys occupied themselves with games and coloring books on the living-room floor, enjoying the presents they had received from their parents that morning.

When everyone was settled, Gideon called his mother, his sisters and Rebecca in from the kitchen where they were putting the finishing touches on the dinner they were about to share. Gideon crossed the room and handed his Bible to Reuben. "Would you read to us the story?"

Everyone grew quiet. Reuben opened the Bible and began in a strong, steady voice to read the Christmas story.

Even the children remained quiet until Reuben finished reading from the second chapter of Luke.

Gideon glanced at Rebecca. She smiled softly at him and he knew it was time. He thanked Reuben and said, "Before we eat, I have a gift for Rebecca." He withdrew a large bundle from inside the closet and carried it across the room to her.

She blushed as everyone looked at her with curiosity. The package was wrapped with plain brown paper and string. Rebecca began to carefully work the string off.

"Me do it." Little Melvin rushed to help. Grabbing the paper, he yanked it apart, smiling at the ripping sound. His mother quickly snagged him and held him in her lap. He protested until his father spoke sternly in his ear.

Rebecca pushed the rest of the paper aside to reveal the quilt she had made. She looked up at Gideon. "You're giving it back to me?"

"I took it under false pretenses. It is your gift to give, and I understand if you wish to give it to someone else."

Everyone laughed. As the families filed into the kitchen, Gideon hung back to speak with Rebecca. "I hope you like your gift."

"I like it, but it belongs to you."

"*Danki.* One day I pray we will share it as husband and wife. Will you marry me, Rebecca?"

"Ja," she answered without hesitation. Her eyes sparkled with her love as she drew his face down for a tender kiss.

"Marry me soon," he whispered. "I can't wait long to make you mine."

"Only a little longer," she promised.

"When?"

"Amish weddings take place in the fall. You know that."

"I can't wait that long."

She drew back and shook her head. "We could have a spring wedding, but you know what folks will think."

"That we've got a babe on the way and need to rush things along."

"Exactly."

"All right, a fall wedding it is, but early fall," he insisted.

"October?"

"September," he countered.

"September," she agreed. He kissed her once more and she settled against his side, more content than she'd been for ten years. God had been good to her.

Gideon laid his forehead against hers. "Do we really have to wait until September?"

"Ja!" a chorus of women's voices answered from the kitchen.

Smiling, Gideon gave Rebecca a quick kiss and together they went in to join the Christmas feast and begin a new life.

* * * * *

Dear Reader,

I hope you enjoyed the story of Gideon's struggle to return to his Amish faith. Both he and Rebecca made bad decisions for the wrong reasons when they were young. Oh, if only we knew at twenty the things we knew by the time we were forty. A lot fewer mistakes might be made.

Life happens, but we don't often get the chance for a do-over. Fortunately, I can give my characters that chance. In the same way, God gives us that chance when we admit our mistakes. We get the chance to wipe the slate clean, to start over with a whole heart and a sense of His purpose in our lives.

By the way, the story of how Adam and Emma Troyer met can be found as a free online read at www.Harlequin.com. Just search the archives for a story called *The Inn at Hope Springs.*

May the Lord bless and keep you and may He shine the light of His love upon you. I wish you all a very merry Christmas and a happy New Year.

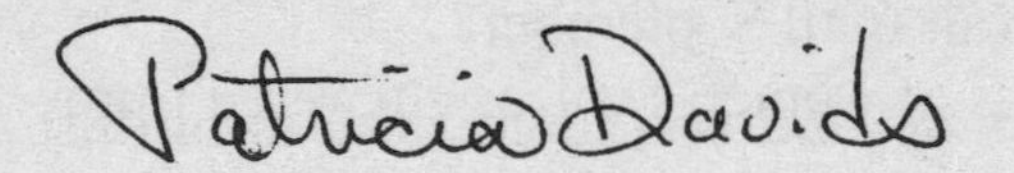

Questions for Discussion

1. Were you surprised to learn that Amish youth participate in wild parties?

2. Was Gideon wrong to keep his identity a secret from Rebecca when they met at the auction? Did you understand his motivation? Why do you feel he was right or wrong?

3. Do you have a past guilt that weighs on your heart? How does that affect your relationship with your family? With God?

4. Rebecca suffered a debilitating and life-changing event when she lost her sight. Do you know someone who is sight-impaired? What is their attitude toward their disability?

5. Did you learn anything new about the Amish in this story?

6. What character did you identify with in this story and why?

7. Do you believe your community would come together to help a member who lost a business the way the people of Hope Springs gathered

around Reuben Beachy when his shop caught fire? Why?

8. The Amish are depicted as leading simple lives. Do you believe this is true or is it merely that it appears that way to outsiders?

9. What part of the story would you like to have changed and why?

10. The practice of shunning is one we find hard to understand. Do you believe it can be helpful for wayward family members or is it a cruel form of punishment?

11. Many people feel Christmas is too commercial. What part of our Christmas traditions would you like to see changed?

12. Gideon gave up flying to return to his faith. What sacrifices have you seen people make in order to become closer to God?

13. Several people have said the Amish seem adept at getting around the restrictions placed on them by their faith, such as hiring drivers instead of owning a car. What do you think of their ability to "bend" the rules? Do you think it diminishes their faith?

14. If you could travel only by horse and buggy, how would that change your life?

15. The Amish clearly face the same challenges and trials that we face. What do you think makes them so strong?